A HEART'S COMPASS
BOOK THREE

USA TODAY BESTSELLING AUTHOR
BROOKE O'BRIEN

UNTIL I FOUND YOU

I've been drowning under the weight of my guilt, pushing away the people I love most to protect them.

Or at least that's what I've been telling myself for five years.

I swore I'd never come back home to Arbor Creek, and to the woman I let slip away. I don't deserve her or her forgiveness, but I'd give my life if it meant keeping her safe.

After I'm forced to return to our small town, I'm faced with the secrets and lies from the past and the demons that kept me shackled for all these years.

When the truth is revealed, she just may be the one who can save me...

Thank you for reading **UNTIL I FOUND YOU**! I hope you love Graham and Halle as much as I do.

You can join my Facebook group, Brooke O'Brien's Rebel Reader Group, to discuss the series and get sneak peeks on future releases. Sign up for my newsletter to find out more about my new releases. To join, please visit: www.authorb rookeobrien.com/follow.

Enjoy the story!

dedication

To my Rebels, thank you for wanting this story.
More importantly, thank you for waiting for it.

chapter one

HALLE

"**W**oah, we're half-way there," I sing, as I furiously massage the conditioner into my hair. "Woah, livin' on a prayer."

I'm not quite sure why I'm singing this song, but it's fitting for this morning. I'm the type of person who sings when I'm trying to focus or when I'm in a hurry. Although I can't sing when I'm trying to read a street sign. I'm one of those people who turns down the radio to see what's fifteen feet in front of me. That's neither here nor there right now.

The point is, I'm running late, and I need all the help I can get. It would come to the surprise of no one that I'm running behind schedule. In fact, if there's one thing you could ever count on, it's that I'm usually two or ten steps behind everyone else.

I get distracted easily, get caught up staring off at whatever shiny object has stolen my attention, like right now. Which is why I'm singing to myself as I stand in the shower, rushing through the process of washing my hair.

I have twenty minutes in which to make it to the Hopeful's Bridal Boutique on the other side of our small town of Arbor Creek. Today is a big day for Ellie, one of my best friends, as she'll hopefully find the dress she's been searching for.

In all honesty, it's not Ellie I'm worried about who will be ticked at me for arriving fifteen minutes past the time I was supposed to be there. No, not at all. It's my roommate and other best friend, Kinsley. She's the yin to my yang. It's what makes our friendship balance out—everything I'm not, she makes up for by pushing me to be.

Kinsley would never be caught dead arriving late for anything. It's more likely she would arrive fifteen to twenty minutes early, with a checklist of everything she needs to do. I'm more of a fly-by-the-seat-of-my-pants kind of girl. I don't have much of my life planned out. I don't even know what I'm going to wear today, let alone have I thought ahead on where I see myself in five years.

I keep Kinsley young and she reminds me to never take life too seriously because, let's face it, we're all going to end up at the same place. I can't take any of this shit with me anyway. I just hope I arrive late when I go too.

Leaning my head back, I let the suds wash away before I run my hand over my long hair, wringing out the water before reaching down to turn off the faucet.

Reaching outside the shower, I blindly pat around for the towel I set on the rack. Grabbing it, I pull it toward me and use it to pat dry my face as the sound of hard knocking pounds against the door.

"Shit. Shit," I groan to myself, realizing I had spent far too much time in the shower. Along with Ellie and Kinsley, our good friend, Brea, who rounds out our little biker gang of badassery is joining us for today. Brea's dating the brother of Ellie's fiancé, so really, she's her sister-in-law for all intents and purposes.

There's a pounding at the door that comes for a second time, spurring me into action. Brea was supposed to be here any minute now, so we could ride together.

Wrapping the towel around my body, I tiptoe my way out of the bathroom and down the hallway. I can imagine the look Kinsley would have on her face if she were to witness this moment, knowing I'm leaving drops of water on the hardwood floor behind me.

This is why we're friends. She needs to learn not to sweat the little things, like water on your floor. It will dry on its own.

Clutching the towel to my chest, I don't bother even looking out the window as I swing the door open and turn back around.

"Hey Brea," I call out over my shoulder, "give me just a second to get dressed, and we'll head out."

Moving quickly, I'm mindful to step around my little puddles of water, careful not to slip and fall, as I head back down the hall toward my bedroom when the sound of his deep voice hits me.

We're usually not prepared for the moments that change our lives. I didn't see it coming the day Graham Shaw broke my heart, shattering it into a million pieces. I thought he was going to be in my life forever, but it turns out forever came sooner than I had expected.

Which brings me to this moment. For a second, I question if this is a cruel version of déjà vu, only now I don't want to believe my ears. Jolting myself into place, I squeeze my eyes shut hoping that what I just heard was all in my head and not at all what I thought it was.

"Do you always open the door to strangers and invite them in, without even checking to see who it is?"

Turning slowly, I wish I would've prepared myself better for what, or rather whom, I was about to see.

My eyes narrow and it takes me a second to collect myself, getting over the shock of seeing Graham Shaw standing before me in all his handsome glory.

"I didn't realize you were a stranger," I bite back, realizing the way he had left me with so many unanswered questions still hits like a hard slap to the face, even after all this time.

My eyes stare intently, as I hold the towel wrapped around me tight. It feels like all the air has been sucked out of the room and of me, reflecting on how much weight is carried in one sentence alone.

If I didn't know any better, I'd say there was a look of guilt that passes over his face, but before I can analyze it further, it's gone. His jaw flexes, as his eyebrows furrow, looking back at me.

I never had expected to be a stranger to Graham, yet now it seems like that's who we are.

It's a weird feeling staring back at the man you loved more than anything. Remembering all the things you knew about him, like the way he used to bite his lip when he was deep in thought or how he'd crack his knuckles when he was nervous.

Looking at the man in front of me, I can't help but feel as though I don't know anything about him. It was hard to get through every day after he left. It almost feels like a lifetime since I last saw him.

Damn, he looks good though. I used to love running my hand over his pecs down to his abs. He always worked out, but when he was younger, he was lean despite years of football and lifting weights. He's filled out more and it pains me to say it, but time was so good to him.

It makes me even more angry to think about all the women he's attracted since then.

"I know you better than you know yourself, Halle. Don't be fooled. I don't understand why the hell you'd open the door and let someone in, not realizing who's on the other side. It's not safe. I could've been anyone."

"First of all, it's been five years. You knew who I was then, but I'm not that girl anymore, Graham. You don't know me at all. Second, if you weren't paying attention when I answered the door, I thought you were my friend, Brea. I didn't think you were just anyone."

His eyebrows raise higher and I realize then if he hadn't felt guilty before, he does now. Maybe even a little shocked too.

"You always were a pain in my ass," he mutters to himself, running a hand over his face and down over his jaw.

In doing so, I watch as he stares back at me and for the first time since walking into my apartment, he lets his eyes roam over my face to my neck and down over the rest of my body. When he finds his way back up, I meet his stare with my eyes narrowed into slits. His stare is so blatant, his eyes burning into every inch of me.

"You used to love that about me," I retort.

A small smile curves at his lips. The mention of the past and what we used to be stings, like a zap to the heart. I had closed all roads to my heart where Graham was concerned a long time ago.

I'm not going down this same road with him again. Not anymore. He had his chance.

"Well, listen, this little reunion has been fun and all, but I have to get going. My friend is gonna be here any minute. So, if you don't mind telling me what the hell you're doing here, that'd be great. That way I can send you back on your way."

The curve of Graham's smile grows, and I want to roll my eyes and demand him to leave.

"Mm, there's the fire," he smirks.

I kid you not, the fucker has the gall to smirk at me. He always loved getting me riled up. I want to smack him upside the head, he makes me so angry.

"Tick, tock. I don't have all day."

"Are you talking back to me right now, Halle?"

"Yes, Graham, that's how conversations with me work. Now get to the point."

Chuckling, he crosses his arms, which leaves me momentarily distracted as my eyes roam over him, taking in the way his muscles bulge when he flexes.

"Kinsley sent me here. Something about helping her roommate load up some things for her for Callum and Ellie's wedding. Do you know anything about that?"

"Kinsley." I pause, feeling the edge of irritation seep into my tone. "I'm sorry, you said Kinsley sent you over here?"

Of course, she did. If there's anyone in my life who hoped Graham and I would end up together, it was Kinsley. In fact, she had our whole wedding planned out for us, knowing exactly every detail we'd want for our big day.

She really missed her calling as an event planner because I swear, the woman is as organized as she is frustrating right now.

"Yeah, I was down at the salon a little bit ago. She helped get me in for a haircut under short notice, so I was doing her this favor in return."

I want to ask him what he's even doing here. Why he's in Arbor Creek when he made it clear when he left that he was never going to return, at least not this soon. As much as it's killing me to ask, I leave it alone.

It's a dead end road and, quite frankly, I don't have it in me to care anymore.

"That's funny, considering Kinsley helped me load everything up last night," I deadpan, looking at Graham unamused.

"Is that right?" He laughs, just as my phone pings with a text message.

Turning on my heel, I continue down the hallway toward my bedroom to grab my phone.

Brea: I'm stuck in traffic on the highway. I'm sorry, I'll have to meet you there.

Ugh! Locking my phone, I toss it absentmindedly somewhere on my bed. Opening my drawer to my dresser, I grab my black lace bra and matching panties. Dropping my towel, I make quick work of putting them on while sauntering across my room toward my closet to figure out what to wear.

Looking in the corner mirror, I see Graham eyeing me from where he still stands rooted in place in our entryway. There's a fire in his gaze, one that's been a long time since I've seen, but remember from all those years ago.

I let him drink me in standing before him, reminding him of everything he let go of when he chose to run away rather than face his problems head on.

It's terrible of me to say, knowing the series of events which led him to leaving, but it doesn't change the fact he hurt me when he did.

Seeing him look at me the same way he did all those years ago lights something within me that's been burned out, withering away for a long time. I've tried to move on, used meaningless relationships with nameless guys as a way of burying my feelings for him.

Staring back at him, I wonder if he's having the same thoughts I am, about how time and distance has changed things between us but the connection between us is still there.

I feel confident and sexy, watching the way his eyes eat up every inch of my body, down to my painted red toes back up over my chest and to my face.

"If that's all, don't let the door hit you on the way out, Graham. Travel safe when you head back to Chicago," I say, opening the closet to search for something to wear.

Peeking my head out from behind the door, I spot Graham reaching down to adjust himself. Biting my lip, I clear my throat as his eyes dart over meeting mine.

"Oh, and do me a favor, will ya?" I smile, loving how wound up he looks, waiting for what I'm about to say.

My smile widens, knowing I have him right where I want him. "Lock the door for me when you go. I wouldn't want anymore strangers showing up at my door and inviting themselves inside."

Leaving him with a wink, I force myself to focus on what I'm doing. I'm glad he can't see me now because my cover would be blown.

I'm so spaced out, thinking about the way he looked at me, that I can't even think straight.

My ears perk, listening for any signs of him leaving. I hear him mutter something about me being a pain in his ass followed by shuffling feet before the door opens. The sounds from outside filter into the apartment and down the hall, then a moment later the door closes once again.

Stepping out from behind the closet door, I take a seat on the edge of the bed and fall back, looking up at the ceiling fan spinning around.

Graham is the only man who's ever made my heart beat out of my chest.

What he's doing back in Arbor Creek, I have no idea, but I'm glad to see him again.

chapter two

HALLE

Leaning over into the trunk of my car, I carefully stack the third box onto the pile before slowly lifting them into my hands. Feeling shaky, I pause and let out a slow breath. I probably should save myself the stress of carrying three boxes of breakables inside, but my momma didn't raise no bitch. Why make two trips when I can get this done in one?

Slowly and carefully, I make my way toward the front of the Hopeful's carrying the boxes of wine glasses and the vases that I ordered on Amazon. The clock is starting to wind down, we're just a couple months away from when Callum and Ellie walk down the aisle.

Taking the step on the curb, I peer into the front of the boutique window and see my girlfriends huddled in a circle. My eyes widen, flashing them with a hard look that says, "one of you pay attention to me and help me open the damn door." As if picking up on my laser focus, Kinsley turns and sees me. Her eyes widen, taking in the stack of boxes in my arms before rushing toward the door to help usher me in.

"What the heck are you doing? You could drop those! And what took you so long to get here?" she mutters, holding the door open for me.

"What are you talking about?" I ask, playing coy. I know she's aware of the fact I'm late. Twenty minutes according to the clock in my car, but I'm playing it off like I'm early. I like to give her hell, it's one of my favorite things to do. Considering she's the reason why Graham showed up at my door this morning, I feel like she deserves it. I'm still not sure if I should be annoyed or mad at her for it yet.

It's why she's my soul mate. She helps balance me out, keep me in line. Most days I love her for it, but days like today when I'm stressed to the max and feeling the error of my ways, I don't want to hear her obvious disapproval.

"We were supposed to be here at nine thirty. It's nine fifty-two, Halle. What took you so long?"

Setting the boxes onto the small table, I turn and face Kinsley.

"What took me so long?" I reply sarcastically. "Well, let's start with the visitor who showed up at my door the moment I was getting out of the shower. Let's start there."

Kinsley looks at me and there's a small grin that stretches across her face.

"I don't know what you're talking about, but I'm glad to see you got the wine glasses and vases here for Ellie to see."

Looking over her shoulder, I see Ellie and Brea standing near a rack of dresses. Kinsley's grandma, June, is sitting in a chair off to the side. She smiles as she watches Ellie hold out each dress she browses.

With an annoyed smile on my face I nod my head. "Wouldn't want to ruin your plans," I retort, waving my hands at her and her notebook. She's been using that thing to call out orders to all of us for the past week. Strolling past Kinsley, I wrap my friend in a hug.

"You look so pretty, Ells. Are you excited to find the perfect dress?"

"Honestly, some of these dresses are so intimidating," she sighs. "I just want something simple. Callum promised me simple."

Ellie doesn't ask for a lot, but the one thing she did say was she wanted a small wedding. She wanted a day filled with all the people she loved as she tied the knot of forever with the only man she's ever loved. Callum, being Callum, promised to give her everything she ever wanted and more. He just wanted to know she was his.

I'm so happy to see someone who deserves it more than anyone finally get her day.

I can't deny the small part of me that feels my heart ache in my chest after seeing Graham today. Five years ago, I thought I found my forever. We were young but were so in love. The two of us together, I thought there was nothing in the world that could tear us apart.

Moments like this, the memories come crashing over me in waves. I find myself doing what I've always done to bury the pain, I find ways of coping, distracting me from the way my heart aches with missing him.

Bringing myself back to the present, I run my hand along Ellie's back before I whisper in her ear, "I promise it will be everything you want and more."

Standing back, I flash Ellie my best smile hoping that it hides my sadness and gives her the reassurance she needs.

"Why don't you show us one of the dresses you have your eye on? Do you have a style you had in mind?"

Kinsley start clapping her hands excitedly.

"Ells, I promise you're going to look stunning." Kinsley walks toward her, reaching over her shoulder to pull a dress off the rack. "I saw you looking at this one. I think you should try it on. Who knows, maybe this is THE dress!"

I take a seat next to June and she reaches over, patting my forearm. "Hi, sweetie, you doin' alright?"

Running my thumb over my fingernail, my mind wanders elsewhere. As soon as I hear the lock on the dressing room door, my eyes shoot up to find Ellie looking stunning in a gorgeous white dress.

It's simple and form-fitting, molding to her body like it was meant for her. Blush highlights her cheeks. She's never liked being the center of attention, but the sparkle in her eye shows just how happy she truly is.

Kinsley lifts the train behind her, using her other hand to help Ellie step onto the platform. We all turn to look in the mirror, searching for any sight of what Ellie may be thinking, but the subtle way she bites her lip shows she's trying to fight back the smile that wants to let loose on her face.

"Ellie, oh my God," Kinsley mutters, pressing her hand to her mouth as tears form in her eyes. I force down the emotion rising in my throat. She looks beautiful.

Ellie's had an incredibly hard life, facing more tragedy and heartbreak than any one person should ever have to endure. Nearly nine months ago, we almost lost her when she was assaulted and abducted. She's fought her way out of that life, and she continues to fight with every ounce of determination in her. No one in this world deserves the happiness she has been given more and seeing how happy she looks in that dress has tears silently streaming down my face.

"What do you think?" Brea asks. Looking around the room, I notice there isn't a dry eye in sight.

"I love it! It's pretty and so perfect. Do you think Callum would like it?"

Ellie bites the inside of her cheek, looking uncertain. There's a hesitancy in her voice, before Kinsley interrupts the seriousness of the moment bursting out laughing.

"Are you kidding? He's going to lose his shit when he sees you walking down the aisle and I can't wait to see it happen."

June laughs softly and I know she, along with the rest of us, agrees with Kinsley's statement. Although I'm positive Callum would be tripping over her no matter what dress she picked.

Ellie quickly swipes away the tear that threatens to fall before she subtlety nods her head agreeing. "I think this is the one then." She smiles. "Oh, God, I'm getting married."

She says the statement with shock underlying her tone, as if she can't believe it's about to happen either.

"You and Callum are going to live a happy life, Ells."

We snap a few pictures of her in the dress, being sure to capture different angles. Holding out my hand, I help her back to the fitting room to change.

Kinsley is back to work looking over the rack of bridesmaid's dresses, so I reassure her I'll help Ellie as she gets the rest of the dresses in order.

I feel her eyes are burning into me, as if she, too, is sensing something is wrong.

"You've been pretty quiet today. It's like your mind is somewhere else. How are you handling everything?" Ellie asks quietly.

"What do you mean?" I question, as she slides the dress down over her hips.

"Brea told us about Graham moving back to town. I figured the news would be hard on you. You don't have to pretend with me though, Halle. I'm here if you ever need to talk."

This is what I love most about Ellie. She's been through so much in her life that she understands the hard. When you need someone to be there for you, not necessarily with the right words to heal you, but just be there for you–it's her.

"I'm sorry, it seems selfish of me. I don't want today to be about me. This is such an incredibly exciting time for you. I promise I'll pull out of my funk. Seeing him earlier was unexpected and more difficult than I ever thought it would be."

"You don't have to worry about that with me, Halle. If there is anyone who understands how you're feeling, it's me. You don't have to pretend around me. Like I said, I'm here for you. You just let me know when you're ready."

I nod. "Thanks, babe." I give her a reassuring smile. She reaches out to grab my hand, squeezing it.

"Now seriously, let's talk about how Callum's going to react when he sees you in this dress. You'd look great in a potato sack, that's why I hate you. He's going to be crying, stumbling over his words. It's going to be adorable." I laugh.

She blushes, her smile growing a mile wide. "That's my plan."

I'd always hoped I'd see Graham again, but having it become reality has me lost in my head. Lost in the past, but I'm doing my best to pull myself out of it. I've been forcing a smile on my face for a long time. I've gotten somewhat good at it by now.

We all have that one person our hearts will always go running back to and, for me, that person will always be Graham. I only wish I were his reason to stay.

chapter three

GRAHAM

The week after seeing Halle was crazy busy. I'm almost thankful for it because it kept my mind occupied. I spent my days preparing for the opening of Compass Security at our new location. My nights were spent with my mother. Her deteriorating health was the reason I was back in Arbor Creek, and I knew she needed me. I made it a point to stop by every night to have dinner or to check in on how she was feeling.

At night, when I was alone in bed, my mind was with Halle. I would lie awake until all hours of the night thinking about her, picturing the look on her face when she turned around to see me standing in her doorway. Even after all these years, time and distance hadn't changed how I felt or the reaction my body had to being near her. All I could think about was pulling her in my arms and never wanting to let her go.

When it was quiet or I was alone in my thoughts, she was all I could think about.

She was always my biggest distraction. I became reckless, going to any lengths to be near her and see her smile. I learned the lesson the hard way when I lost my cousin, Gage.

The guilt I felt over knowing it was me who put him on the road the night of his accident was never far from my mind.

When I got a phone call from Detective Keller asking for me to stop down at the police station, it was like a flashback to the night he died. I was brought back to the feelings I had when I heard his screams, the painful ache in my chest when I saw his body being pulled from the totaled car, and the heart shattering words of being told he was gone.

"Hello, my name is Graham Shaw. I have an appointment at ten to meet with Detective Keller."

The secretary's eyes light up when she sees me. I smile at her as she turns her attention back to her computer, her fingers clicking at a furious speed.

"Thank you, Mr. Shaw. Go ahead and take a seat. I'll let Detective Keller know you're here and he'll be right with you."

"Great." I smile, taking a seat in the chairs lining the room. I wince at the ache in my lower back, trying to get comfortable. It was a long night last night. My back is sore from sleeping in the recliner at my mom's all night.

My mom's health has recently taken a turn for the worse. When she called to tell me she had been admitted into the hospital a few months ago, I knew it was time to come home. It was something I never thought I would be doing but she needed me closer to help her. She gave up her life to take care of me and I knew it was time I repaid her.

Besides my friends who had become like family to me, she was all I had.

Dean, my business partner, and I decided it was time we take things another step forward with Compass Security. Opening another location in Everton, a town outside of Arbor Creek, allowed me to be closer to my mom.

I hope nights like last night come few and far between or I'm going to have to invest in a new bed in my old bedroom. Sleeping in the recliner just isn't for me. I'd do anything to be there for her, helping take care of her. If I could take away her pain, I would do it in a heartbeat.

"Mr. Shaw, thank you for coming by."

Jarring me from my thoughts, I glance up at the man standing in front of me. He's dressed in a dark navy button up shirt and tan dress slacks, with a badge hanging from his waist.

Standing, I reach my hand out to him and shake it.

"No problem." I was taken by surprise when I got the phone call from the local detective shortly after arriving in town. He hadn't given me much information, just simply asked if I could stop down at the police station to talk to him.

"If you don't mind me asking, what's this about?"

As much as I'm grateful for the pleasantries and all, I prefer to get to the point. My priority was making sure my mom was taken care of, but I still struggled to get my mind off why they asked me to stop by. I hadn't been in town in over five years.

What could they need to talk to me about now, after all this time? If it was so important, why hadn't they reached out to me sooner?

"Let's go into my office, shall we? That way we have a little more privacy, and we can sit down and talk through this."

Nodding my head, I follow along behind him. He shuts the door behind me, motions to the seats facing the large oak desk, and urges me to take a seat.

"I appreciate you stopping down here today."

Folding my hands together, I nod my head, hoping to encourage him to continue.

Coming back to Arbor Creek has been incredibly difficult. It's drudged up a lot of painful memories I would've preferred to keep buried.

"The reason I called you down here today is because there's been an update in your cousin's case."

My brows furrow, confused. I'll be honest, I wasn't even aware Gage's accident was even considered an open case. To my knowledge, it had been ruled a hit and run. They couldn't determine who the driver was, and after investigating it for months after I had left for Chicago, I figured they had focused their attention elsewhere.

"Really?"

"When we had last spoken, following the accident, we believed your cousin had been hit by a drunk driver who had fled the scene of the accident. For months, we investigated it and were unable to locate any witnesses or pinpoint any clues that could tie someone to the scene that night.

"When Gage was hired on, he had been working on a case for us involving two brothers. Isaac and Marc Krate. Are you familiar with them?"

Who isn't? Arbor Creek isn't a big town. Everyone knows everyone.

More like everyone is in everyone's business. The Krate brothers have made a name for themselves around here as being a couple of scumbags, honestly. Last I had heard, they had been involved in drugs passing through Arbor Creek to Des Moines.

"Yes. I'm aware of them and some of the things they were up to back then," I say.

"Well, in that case, I'm sure you're aware your cousin was one of the officers responsible for putting Isaac Krate in prison on felony drug charges."

I was aware, but I guess I'm not sure what that has to do with Gage's accident.

"We believe that your cousin's accident may not have actually been an accident. We don't know for certain yet, we're still looking into it, but I understand that you've moved back to town and with the nature of your business, I felt it was necessary to tell you. We have reason to believe it may have been his brother, Marc, who caused the crash."

My jaw locks as tears sting my eyes. Even after Gage had died, I hadn't cried. I sat through his funeral and watched as his mom crumbled on the floor near his casket, weeping over the loss of her son. I watched as the pallbearers carried him from the hearse to the grave site and lowered him into the cold, hard earth.

I went through the motions of packing up my bags, my life, and said goodbye to the people closest to me because

I believed they deserved a life without me around. A life where my decisions didn't put them at risk too.

Sitting here in front of this man, I feel the tears fill my eyes and the urge to cry, but I don't.

Taking a deep breath, I let the oxygen fill my lungs as I slowly release it.

"What does this mean?"

"I'm sorry, I know this is upsetting to hear. With you being back in Arbor Creek, we felt it was important you knew. We believe this was done in retaliation for Gage's involvement in putting Isaac in prison. Right now, we don't have enough evidence to arrest him. Gage was my friend, Graham, and like you, I want justice for him. If this was out of revenge, I wanted you to know so you can keep your eye out and stay safe."

"Why do you think Marc was responsible? What do you have on him?"

"That I can't say," he says, not giving me anything more.

Flexing my jaw, I know he's not going to give any more details away.

"You bring me down here and tell me all of this, but you can't tell me why you think it's him?"

"This is still considered an ongoing investigation, Graham. Sharing anymore information I have right now could hinder the chance of us putting him away. I need you to trust me."

I can feel heat under my skin, the anger building up. Pressing my lips firmly, I nod my head in agreement.

"Promise me you will leave this to us," he commands.

Gage had so much of his life ahead of him when he was ripped from this world. Even though I've thought about this a million times and told myself he wouldn't want me to feel the way I do I carry a tremendous amount of guilt over my decisions being what led him to be on the road that night.

They were my decisions that led to the accident and where he is now.

Gage grew up wanting to be a police officer. It was all he had talked about from the time we were young. I remember watching him play Cops and Robbers with his friends. Gage, without fail, was always the good guy. He wanted to be the one that protected people, especially the ones he loved. I wanted to honor him by doing the same thing. Gage was more of a big brother to me than my cousin.

"The minute anything changes, I want to be the first person you call."

I curl my hands into fists, tension coiling in my body. Everything in me wants to grab him by the neck and demand he let me help, but it is futile.

I need to trust they are doing everything they can to investigate this and put the person responsible for killing Gage behind bars.

Reaching my hand out, I shake Keller's and we both agree if we hear anything more, we'll be in touch. As soon as I step out the door, I unlock my phone and press the button connecting the call to Dean.

"What'd they have to say?"

"Remember how before Gage died, Isaac Krate had been arrested for drug trafficking?"

"They think it's connected to what happened to him?"

"He wouldn't tell me what evidence they have, but they think Marc Krate has something to do with Gage getting run off the road that night."

"Motherfucker," he curses.

Opening the door to my truck, I climb in and turn the ignition. Leaning back against the seat, I run my fingers through my hair and scrub my palms over my face.

"Graham, I've told you from day one this wasn't your fault. I still believe that today."

"Dean." I cut him off, not wanting to hear it.

"No," he stops me, raising his voice. "You listen to me. This wasn't your fault and it's time you stop punishing yourself like it was. No one, certainly not Gage, would want you to continue to put this on yourself the way you have been."

"Alright," I say, hoping it will get him to stop. We've been through this hundreds of times. Nothing he says now is going to change how I feel.

"I've gotta go. I need to head down to the office."

"Yeah, okay," he says, sighing in frustration. "Do me a favor, will ya?"

"Shoot."

"You're home now. I know being close to Halle again is probably stirring up old emotions. I'm sure you've convinced yourself you don't deserve her. Just do me a favor. Promise me you'll take a chance to have a conversation with her and tell her how you feel."

"Dean," I warn. "Halle and I were over years ago. It's better this way."

"I don't think, for a second, you believe the bullshit you're spewin'. Do yourself a favor, don't push her away anymore."

GRAHAM

Knocking on the door twice, I turn the knob and push it open a crack. "Mom, you home?" I don't know why I bother asking if she's home. I saw her car when I pulled around the back alley, and I can hear the TV on in the living room, but I ask anyway.

"Hi, honey," she sings. Her voice doesn't sound the same as it once did when I was growing up. There is a harshness to her tone, a sad realization every time I hear her that I'm losing another person I love. It makes me feel terrible when I see her, knowing she had been living through this and didn't want to burden me with her health concerns.

I slip off my shoes near the door and take the steps two at a time until I reach the landing in our old split-foyer home. The smell of my childhood home still hits me and just like that I'm seventeen years old, living life without a care in the world.

Except things are so different now than they were back then. Life isn't as easy in the real world as it is when you're living at home with your mom and she does everything she can to keep you safe from the reality living outside your window. As much as she tried, she couldn't protect me from everything though. Death doesn't discriminate, and karma has a way of sending you your dues when you least expect them.

Stepping into the living room, I see the shadow of my mom's hands on the carpet of the rug in the middle of the living room. The sunshine peeking in through the window add light to where she sits in her recliner focusing on another one of her knitting projects.

"Hi, sweetheart. I didn't expect you today. What are you doing here?" she wheezes.

"I was going to stop by and get the yard mowed for you and wanted to check on how you were doing on food in the house. I was gonna pick up some groceries for the weekend, and I thought I could pick you up a few things too."

Her scoff comes out more like a cough as she peers up at me. The tubes wrapped around her face helping her to breathe leave me with a weight on my chest realizing once again how different things are.

"Oh honey, you didn't have to do that. I still have leftover casserole in the freezer that will get me by for the next couple of days. I don't want you fussing over me."

"I'm not fussing over you, Ma. I'm just making sure you're taken care of. I'm in town now and I'm going to keep taking care of you, so please let me. Okay?"

It's been a constant back and forth between us getting her to accept any help.

"Okay, dear, I'm sorry. It's an adjustment seeing you come around so much. I know you're busy getting things up and running over there at your new business. I don't want your old ma to be a thorn in your side. How are things, by the way? I heard you on the phone the last time you were over here; sounds like there were some troubles."

Her hands continue to shake as she glances back down at the needle, wrapping another piece of yarn around it before doing the same to the other side. My eyebrows pinch together listening to her talk.

I know if I don't tell her what's going on, she'll only push me to tell her. If I'm talking, that means she's quietly listening, so I take a seat across from her on the couch and tell her everything that's going on.

We are only a couple weeks away from our opening and we've already managed to land several large clients, leading to us opening another branch in the Chicago area. Dean and I both agreed with my mom's health declining, it only made sense for me to run the Everton branch while he stayed back in Chicago and worked with Craig to get the Chicago location off the ground.

"You've accomplished so much for yourself. Your aunt Samantha and I are so proud of you. I know Gage would be proud of you too."

It's the first time in a long time I've heard her say his name out loud. Hearing her say his name brings me back to all those years ago when we would sit right here, playing Grand Theft Auto on my PlayStation. I would give anything, even my very own life, to have him here today.

"Thanks, Mom. Means a lot," I say, choking out the last part. Her praise is hard to hear and even harder to accept with the weight of Gage's memory associated to it. He wanted to protect people, so in my own way I like to believe I'm giving back what he didn't have the opportunity to give himself.

"Have you spoken to Halle since you've been in town?"

As if feeling the whiplash from Gage's name a moment ago, hearing her mention Halle feels like my heart was ripped from my chest.

There are a lot of things I regret when it comes to me and Halle, especially how I ended things with her. She didn't deserve for me to treat her the way I did, but I also know there would have been no easy way for me to walk away from her. I deserved for her to hate me just the same as I hate myself.

"Nah," I say, my own word coming out hoarse. I want to end this conversation as quickly as possible. Talking about Gage and then Halle is not something I've mentally prepared myself for, so I do my best to change the subject.

Pressing my palms to my knees, I move to stand. I can feel my mom's eyes on me as she follows me into the kitchen. I busy myself with looking through the cupboards, making a mental list of all the things I want to pick up for her. I'm so lost in my own thoughts I don't even hear the back door open until the soft echoing of her voice floats through the room.

"Good afternoon, Sandy."

Her voice sounds like a song. It's like I've swallowed a bag of cotton, trying to force myself to breathe as I squeeze my eyes closed. My entire body is tense, my shoulders and back straight like my spine was replaced with a metal rod.

I force my feet to move, shuffling enough for me to glance over my shoulder toward the direction of where her voice came.

When my eyes fall on her, it's like I've taken a heavy shoulder to the chest in football. Only this time, there is no pads covering my body. She knocks the wind right out of me with her beauty, just like she did all those years ago.

Her blonde hair is curled in soft waves, pulled over to the side, hanging over her shoulder. I notice the length, how much longer it is since we were younger. I used to pull up her profile on Facebook, but after the last time when I found she removed me from her friends list, I chucked my phone against my dorm room wall and couldn't bring myself to pull it back up.

Her eyes look bold and bright, her eyelashes so long and her smile so inviting, it nearly takes every ounce of strength in me not to pull her into my arms. Everything about her reminds me of the girl I once knew, but where we are today reminds me how wrong that assumption is.

As soon as her eyes fall on mine, they widen in shock. She clearly didn't expect to see me, which brings me to wondering what she's doing here anyway.

"Halle, is that you?" My mom's voice calls out from the living room. I blink through the confusion; her eyes bounce between me and the other room before landing back on mine.

"What are you doing here?" I ask, at the same moment she says, "You're here."

I want to ask her to say something again, simply plead with her to speak so I can hear her voice. Let her words run through me like a balm to my battered heart, but I don't. I don't deserve it, just like I don't deserve to have her in my life.

I have to keep reminding myself that while I'm living here because I know how easy it would be for me to give in and let her back into my life.

"Of course, I'm here. I grew up here, this is my mom's house. What are you doing here?" I ask, repeating my question, only this time the words come out harsher. My hands itch to pull her closer to me, to touch her tanned skin to see if it's as soft as I remember it being beneath my fingers.

The look on her face transforms right before my eyes, likely from hearing the bitterness in my voice.

"I've been coming over here once a week for as long as I can remember, but somehow this is the first time in years I've seen you here. Have you given your mom the same conversation about not leaving her door unlocked and open for strangers?"

My jaw ticks. There's a hint of annoyance, but I want to smile at her sassy remark she's throwing back at me.

"Graham, who are you talking to in there?"

I hear the footrest of her recliner close, knowing she's likely coming to find out what's going on. I take a few steps to peer around the corner into the living room, checking on her.

"Ma, it's fine. You don't need to get up. Halle is here; she said she came over to see you."

I flash Halle a look that says our conversation earlier is not over, at least not yet. She returns it with a sarcastic smile before following behind me into the living room. She graces her with one of her warm smiles. My heart aches to be on the receiving end of one of those smiles again.

"How are you doing, Ms. Sandy? I thought I'd stop by and finish pulling those weeds. I got most of them done in the front but thought since it's cooler out today I'd get a head start on the backyard. I just wanted to check on you before I did, see if you needed anything."

"Thank you so much, sweetie. It's so good to see you. I was hoping you'd stop by and tell me how your day with Ellie and the girls went."

"It went amazing. Ellie found the perfect dress. I can't wait for you to see her. Callum is going to lose it when he sees her. She looked beautiful."

Listening to Halle talk to my mom makes me realize how much I've missed being gone. She always loved Halle, that much was very apparent even when we were young. Anytime she would come over, she would immediately walk to the kitchen to greet her with a smile and a hug. Hearing them talk now though, it's different. Their bond has grown, and I know a lot of that has to do with me being gone.

Listening to Halle talk to my mom about wedding dress shopping is too much for me. I decide I need to get out of here fast.

"I'm going to leave you two. Ma, I'll be outside getting started on the yard. I'll come back in before I take off to the store."

Halle doesn't look back at me as I pass by her. There's a part of me that wonders if she's thinking the same thing I am. I always hoped down the road it would be us talking about wedding planning, but things have changed since then.

Taking a step back out onto the back deck, I feel the wooden boards creak beneath my footsteps as I make my way down the stairs and out toward the shed. I busy myself with starting the mower and put in my earbuds, wanting to drown out the memory of Dean and his comments about pushing Halle away again.

Knowing she's going to be starting in the backyard, I knock out that first so when she comes outside, I can focus on the front without having her near me. It's simply better if we're not around each other, I tell myself over and over. This is the way it has to be.

The sun beats down on me as Luke Combs blares loudly in my ears. A little while later, with the sweat trickling down my face and over my arms, I cut the engine on the mower and push it back to the shed. Closing the padlock, I use the bottom of my T-shirt to wipe the moisture from my face.

As soon as I let go of the cotton material, my eyes fall on Halle. Her eyes are on me, too, but instead they are staring heavily at my abs that are now covered by the T-shirt. Her eyes trail a path down my legs and back up my body to my face. Once they do, I expect her to shy away from the fact that she has now been caught checking me out, but no.

Not Halle.

Clearing my throat, I expect her to avoid any conversation, but she doesn't. Instead she keeps her eyes focused on me, looking me straight in the eye.

"Can I help you?"

"Excuse me?" she retorts.

"Well, from the way you were just looking over here, I thought maybe you had something to say. Something on your mind."

She barks out a laugh, using the back of her gloved hand to cover her mouth. There's mud on her cheek and covering her gloves, as a pile of weeds sit next to her on the ground. Her tan legs are covered in dirt and I keep my eyes trained on her face to avoid staring at the way her muscles in her legs flex when she moves.

"Graham, I truthfully don't have anything more to say to you. I don't know how long you're in town for; I don't expect it will be long before you're running off again. Just because I can appreciate a good view doesn't mean I want anything more from you. That ship sailed a long time ago."

Hearing her admit out loud she's no longer interested burns, but in a way I'm glad. It will make it easier knowing she doesn't want anything to do with me. This is what I wanted, right? The goal was to push her away, and it looks like I am successful in doing so.

"That's good to hear, actually. Although for a different reason."

For a second, if I'm not mistaken, a look of hurt flashes over her face.

"Hate to break it to you," I chide. "but I'm not actually going anywhere. I'm home, so it looks like you'll get a whole lot more of this view than you were expectin'."

chapter five

HALLE

God, I just wanted to smack him across his handsome face for what he said when we were outside. He knew what he was doing trying to get a rise out of me, only now it was different. It made want to slap him even more.

It had felt like forever since we were together in this house. There were so many nights I'd lay in my bed with my eyes closed trying to picture him and all the times we were together. I remember the way our eyes would always find each other's, even in a crowded room. It was like there was a string tying my body to his, keeping us tethered together.

Being near him now, even in the quietness of his mom's house after all this time, I still find myself wanting to walk across this room and wrap my arms around his waist, press my face against his chest, and inhale his clean scent.

Sometimes, in my dreams, I'd swear I could smell him. It seems crazy to say this, but there were times I'd wake up expecting to find him at the foot of my bed, the scent was so strong. Those were the nights when the dreams seemed so real, it's like they were haunting me.

In the beginning, I couldn't come around Sandy or this house without the sadness I felt nearly crippling me.

So, I wasn't proud of who I was after that. I would've given anything to make those feelings go away. I just wanted to have someone look at me the same way Graham did, so I searched for it, through meaningless relationships. I'd drink my way through bottle after bottle, hoping to find what I was looking for at the bottom. Hoping to numb my pain, but it never worked. Going home with nameless strangers never helped either.

I sent him texts for almost a year, telling him how much I loved him, how I would never give up on him or us, and when he was ready to come home, I'd be here for him waiting.

Thinking about it now, I wonder if he ever read those messages.

Using the back of my arm, I wipe the strand of blonde hair that has fallen from my ponytail and brush it back away from my face. Reaching over, I turn on the sink testing the water temperature before pumping soap onto my hands.

I close my eyes for a second, rubbing my hands together as I let my mind wander back to our conversation outside.

I don't hear him come up behind me over the sound of the water splashing against the sink. When he clears his throat, I know he's wondering what I'm doing.

"You alright?" he asks, his eyebrows furrow as he looks over my face, checking to make sure there are no signs that something is wrong.

I run my hands under the water, before turning it off and grabbing two paper towels from the counter to dry them.

"Yeah, I'm fine. Just a long day is all, and I still have to get to the salon after this."

"Salon, huh? I was there the other day, saw it when Kinsley gave me a haircut. Mason told me about it a while back, said Hudson was proud of you two. How he was going around town singing his praises over all you had accomplished."

My smile warms my face thinking about Kinsley's grandfather and his pride he's always had for all of us.

"Yeah, we opened it last year. It's been going well actually, I love it. It's what makes me happy."

His eyes focus on my mouth for a moment, which only makes me more conscious of it. I force my mouth to close, biting on my lip. Graham clears his throat, clenching his hands together before he glances back at me.

"Listen Hals, um–Halle, I had no idea you had been coming by here and doing work for my mom." His face softens and I know, even after our little tiff we had outside, he appreciates me looking out for her. "You really didn't have to do that, but I'm glad you were there for her when I wasn't. I don't know what she had you doing or if you had to spend any of your own money, but if you did please let me know. I have no problem paying you back for whatever you've spent helping her around the house, picking up stuff from the store. I'm back home now though, so I can take over, so you don't have to. I'm sure you have other things, other people you'd rather be spending your time with."

My eyes narrow at him. I know he means well, he just wants to show his appreciation, but it ticks me off at the same time. Taking the paper towels in my hand, I crumple them up in my fist, clenching it.

"Graham, I didn't do that for you. I did that for her. I wasn't the only person you chose to run out on when you left for Chicago, not bothering to care what it did to us here. I came by because I knew she missed you and could use the help. After a while, it just became our routine. I'd stop by, help her do some things around the house, have lunch with her, or pick up a few things she needed from the store. You don't owe me a penny, nor do you need to be concerned with who I spend my time with, whether it's your mother or someone else. I bet it won't be long now before you get busy with your new business or decide your time is up here. She'll need my help again, so if it's alright with you, I'd like to keep up with the routine we've had worked out."

"Well, see, that's the thing," he sighs, running his hand along the back of his neck.

He always did that when he was tense or feeling stressed, which makes me wonder what else he has weighing on his mind. It's none of my business though; he's proven for a long time he doesn't need me being there to help him through. "I'm not going anywhere, Halle. What's it gonna take to get you to believe me?"

I chuckle softly to myself. There were years I hoped this day would come, that Graham would tell me he's here to stay, but somehow hearing it now, it's different. I almost wish he would go to avoid the pain of having to be around him again while not being able to hold him.

"I don't believe you for a second, but for your mom's sake, I hope it's the truth. Like I said, I didn't do this for you. I stopped caring what you wanted or made you happy a long time ago."

After leaving Sandy's house, I decided to go for a drive and blare some music before I head into the salon for the day. I had some time to spare before my first client and while I had things I could get done, I needed some time to collect my thoughts. Going for a long drive was one of the few ways I've been doing that nowadays.

Something about rolling down your windows, turning up the music, and taking the back roads around this town was soothing to my soul. I sang Miranda Lambert so loud I couldn't even think about how much I missed Graham. For a second, with the wind blowing through my hair, it almost seemed like the weight of missing him all these years was gone too.

Going into the salon, I knew if I couldn't get my mind right Kinsley would pick up on something being wrong. I still wasn't ready to tell her about seeing him, even if I knew sooner or later it was going to happen.

Driving down the alley behind the salon, I pull into my parking spot and put it into park. I run my fingers through my messy strands. I should be thankful the messy, beachy waves is the style now. My windblown hair almost looks like this was intentional.

Sliding my purse over my shoulder, I swipe my lip gloss over my lips. On a normal day, I would run home and take a quick shower after working out in the yard but it's a short day and I plan on having a night in tonight, so I didn't bother.

"Hals, that you?" The door chimes as I enter through the side door, alerting her of my arrival.

"Yeah, Kins. It's me."

I make a beeline for the back room to drop off my purse, but I don't even make it through the doorway when her head pops in behind me.

"You alright?"

I swear, there is no one on this earth who knows me better than Kinsley Hudson. She's like my soul sister and I love her deeply, but today is one of those days I wish she couldn't read me like a book.

"Of course," I say, putting extra emphasis on my chipper tone hoping to throw her off.

I glance at her over my shoulder. Her hand is perched on the side of the door and her eyes narrow, looking at me. Her laser like stare burns holes into me, and I want to tell her to knock it off.

"You're not fooling me. Try again. What happened?"

"Can we talk about it later? I'm not sure I am ready to talk about it yet."

She pauses, as if she's not sure if this is one of those moments where she should press further hoping she can get it out of me knowing talking about it will help make me feel better or if I truly need her to give me the time.

I don't know one way or another myself because I'm not sure if I'll ever be ready to talk about Graham being back in town and how I'm going to force myself to live my life like he's not.

"I'll give you some time because I think it's what you need, but not too much. We're going to talk before we leave tonight, alright? So, whatever is going on in that pretty head of yours, I'll help you with it here in a bit."

She doesn't give me a chance to reply, as she spins on her heel and walks right back out. Who am I kidding though? If she wants to talk about it, we're gonna talk about it. There's no way around it.

Over the next couple of hours, I busy myself with my clients. I was happy because one of my friends from a few towns over, Ryan, stopped by. She's the girlfriend of Graham's friend, Maverick. I always love catching up with her. Her sassy and spunky personality is just what I needed to pull me out of my earlier mood.

We spent a couple of hours together, dying her hair and trimming it. While I hadn't expected it, she asked me if I had a chance to see Graham recently, and I could once again feel Kinsley's eyes staring at me as I nodded my head at Ryan in the mirror. She knew about the first time, seeing as she helped orchestrate it, but by how she's looking at me now it's obvious she knows it's not the only time.

Ryan picks up on it being a subject I'd rather not talk about and doesn't ask anything more, instead moves on to share how Mav has been working with Graham. I wasn't the least bit surprised.

Maverick and Graham were as thick as thieves growing up. He lived a few towns over where Gage, Graham's cousin, lived. Although they didn't see each other often, I know how much their friendship meant to Graham. It's how he met

Dean, so I guess it only makes sense Maverick would be helping them get their company up and running.

By the time Ryan took off, I was worn down and ready to shower, put on my pj's and watch a movie with a glass of wine. I was hoping Kinsley would see it and give me a break, but when she walked out of the back room a few minutes later I knew there was no chance.

"Sit, you look tired as hell."

Well, at least she can still read me even if she isn't going to cut me some slack.

"You saw Graham again? Why didn't you tell me?"

"It's part of the reason why I didn't want to talk earlier. I knew he was back, but I still don't think I was ready to be around him. Just like I don't think I'm ready to talk about it right now. It's not like I can avoid him though. Arbor Creek is a small town, I'm bound to run into him at some point. I guess I just need to rip off the Band-Aid already."

She nods her head and I can sense the sympathy. Walking toward me, she wraps her arms around my shoulders and pulls me into a hug.

"You know it's going to get better, right?" she mumbles into my ear. "It's not always going to feel like this. You're so strong, Hals. You'll be happy again."

Tears prick my eyes as I blink through them, not wanting to let my emotions get to me. I don't try to speak though, so I simply respond with a nod.

We stand like this for a minute and when I let out a heavy sigh, she finally releases me enough to step back to make sure I'm okay.

"I know I will. I just felt like seeing him was like reopening an old scar. I just need to stop thinking about the past, the what could've been. I need to stop touching the wound because there's no way I'm going to heal if I don't."

Shuffling through a stack of papers, I search for the one I need. I knew I should've hired an assistant when Dean brought up the question, but we didn't need the extra expense right now.

Getting Compass Security up off the ground after returning home has not been easy, especially when my business partner, Dean, is working seven hours away in Chicago. Having an assistant would really come in handy right now.

I was up late last night with my mom. Her blood sugar dropped, I was worried to leave her unattended. I opted to sleep on my old twin mattress. It was my only option if I had any hope of getting a wink of sleep at all.

Two knocks sound on the door and I glance up to see Maverick, my best friend and associate, standing in front of me.

"Dude, you alright?" he asks.

I watch as he adjusts his position where he stands, leaning against the door frame, eyeing me as I shuffle through the papers strewn all over my desk.

I'm a mess. This office is a mess. Everything is a fucking mess.

"Yeah, if I could only find the fucking paper with the—ah! Here it is," I sigh, falling back into my seat in relief.

Maverick and I have been friends since we were young. I grew up living in Arbor Creek, which is where I went to high school. When I wasn't staying at home with my mom, I was likely in Everton staying with my aunt Samantha. Most of our time was spent down at the local skatepark with my cousin, Gage. It's where I met Dean and Maverick.

"How is your mom doing?" Mav asks, crossing his arms in front of him.

"She didn't get much sleep last night. I ran home to shower and change this morning, so I stopped by on my way into the office and she had fallen back asleep. I'm going to stop over again on lunch to check on her."

"Well, if you need anything man, just let me know. You've been there for me a lot this past month," Maverick says. "You tend to focus on everyone else around you, but you know I got your six."

Maverick has had enough of his own shit to worry about without me burdening him with my problems. Serving his second tour in Afghanistan, he got a call his father had passed. He returned home early to take care of everything. Nothing could've prepared him for the shit he was leaving behind him. What they thought was the end of their tour ended with him receiving a call informing him his team had been hit by a roadside bomb. He lost half his platoon.

The two of us combined have lost our fair share of people close to us. It's a constant reminder to never take life for granted.

The sound of my phone rings and immediately thinking of my mom, I swipe it from where it sits on my desk. When I see the name, I know it's important too.

"I'm gonna take this," I say, motioning to Maverick.

Looking up at Maverick, he nods his head as I answer the call.

"G, I got some news for you."

"What do ya know?"

"I got a call a few minutes ago. Krate was spotted outside of Brodie's last weekend. I don't know what it was about, my informant couldn't say, but I know he was meeting with one of Hendrich's guys."

"Fuck!" I grunt. Hendrich is known for his sketchy past. Just last month he was in jail for drug related charges.

"I know, man. It's only a matter of time though. He'll fuck up and we'll catch him."

"Yeah, but how many other lives are at risk having that son of a bitch out on the streets. He deserves to be locked behind bars and to know he's fucking around with Hendrich further proves so."

"I hear ya, man. I'll stay in touch with my contact and keep you in the loop if I hear anything else."

Hanging up the phone, I yell for Maverick to come back in my office.

"What was that about?"

"Turns out Krate is back into some bullshit."

I know Maverick understands the weight of what I'm saying. I was the one who put Gage there that night, but Krate is still responsible for his own actions.

"We will get him, G. It'll happen."

"I want you to keep on him for me. If you hear anything, let me know. I have to check on my mom, make sure she's alright," I say, picking up my baseball cap off the coat rack behind me.

"Oh, and do me a favor, do something about those papers on my fucking desk. Will ya?"

With the sound of his laugh behind me, I duck my head from the sun as I head out the door.

It's after seven o'clock when I finally make it out of the office and home for the night. Running on six hours of sleep, the smart decision would be for me to go home and call it a night. Then, there's the other side of me, the one thinking about the text about going to Brodie's tonight that's winning out. A group of my friends are going out tonight to celebrate Callum and Ellie's engagement. Knowing Halle will be there and the thought of seeing Halle again is the reason why I head home to change out of my work clothes instead of putting on some gym shorts and a movie.

It's been weeks since I've seen her, but the thought of her walking down the hall in nothing but her towel is not something that's been far from my mind. It's made it hard to fall asleep every night.

She's done a good job of evading me around town, for the most part. I know she's been by to see my mom a couple of times. I've noticed the yellow daisies sitting on the table, her favorite flower. When I went back last week, there were two cupcakes on a plate in the kitchen. My mom insisted she brought one by for the two of us.

It's a quarter to nine when I pull up to Brodie's. Parking out back, I walk in through the side door. I spot Mason and Callum standing near the bar, along with our friends, Brannon and Wes.

"Look who decided to finally come hang out with his friends!" Callum shouts over the loud music. His broad grin takes over his face. Happiness looks good on him.

I'm surprised when I don't see any of the girls standing around them. I knew coming out tonight was going to put me right back to where we were in high school. My eyes survey the crowd at the bar tonight. It doesn't take long before my eyes fall on the beautiful long blonde hair and sun-kissed skin I know belong to Halle. She's standing next to Kinsley and Ellie, who I had a chance of meeting when I had to stop out at Callum's place earlier this week to help install a security system.

It takes work, but I force my eyes away from her and back to Callum.

"What's up, man? I guess I should officially congratulate you now." I smile. It's the first genuine smile I've felt in a while and I feel the weight of the bullshit going on ease a little bit.

"Thanks, brother. Who would've thought I'd be the first one to officially tie the knot?"

He's right though, even if it's hard to hear. I'm reminded again Halle's not too far from me. Remorse is written all over Callum's face, showing he hadn't intended for it to come across like it had sounded.

Reaching out, I clap my hand on Callum's back and con-gratulate him again. Even if the past keeps getting thrown back in front of me, I genuinely am happy for my friend.

"Well, look who it is!" Her loud cheerful voice booms from behind me. Stepping back from Callum, I turn to see Kinsley with her chocolate brown hair curled over her shoulder holding a shot of what appears to be whiskey in her hand.

I can feel Halle's eyes on me. Our bodies have always been so in tune with one another. I do my best to not turn my head and look at her. The fear of not knowing what look I'll find staring at me is what has me resisting.

Reaching my arms out, I pull Kinsley into a close hug.

"It's good to see you again," she murmurs in my ear, low enough for only me to hear over the crowd of people and music blaring through the speakers.

"It's good to see you too. Oh, and just so you know, I'm getting you back for that little run-in you planned," I quip. Outside of sending her a text message calling her a "little shit" I never did mention to her what her little surprise led to.

She barks out a loud laugh. "Yeah, I heard all about it. Consider myself punished." She giggles.

"How's she doing?" I ask. If there's anyone who knows and understands the depth of what Halle meant to me, it's Kinsley.

"Better now. She won't say it, but I know she's glad you're home."

"I missed you, Kins."

"I missed you, too, you big lug. Don't you think about leaving again either or I'll be hauling ass out of this town and will drag you back here with me."

She laughs. It's light and joking, but I don't doubt for a second if I were to try and leave again, she really would come after me.

Despite how hard it has been for me to be back, the desire to leave again isn't there. I know Gage would've wanted me home.

"Alright, everyone," Kinsley announces, with her hands cupped around her mouth. "I have an announcement to make."

Stepping back, I let my eyes fall around the group again, but it doesn't take long before they fall on Halle. The moment I look at her, I'm surprised when I find hers looking back at me as if she's been waiting for the moment I give in and look at her.

The small smile that curves the edge of her lip draws my attention down to it, making it difficult to not interrupt the announcement and pull her close to me. I don't though, because as much as I want her, I know I don't deserve her after all the hurt I've caused.

Flashing her a wink, I turn my attention to Kinsley and the tray of shot glasses on the table.

"We are all here tonight to celebrate our good friends, Callum and Ellie, on their engagement. Ellie, we are all so happy you found your way to Arbor Creek, but there is no one here more thankful than Callum. We are so happy for you both and to be a part of the big day. When we decided to get together to plan your bachelor and bachelorette parties, we knew there was no way Callum would let you go far without him being close behind." Kinsley laughs, looking over to where Callum stands, his arm wrapped around his fiancée's waist as his nods his head in agreement.

He leans down, whispering something in her ear. Whatever he said must've been only for them to hear, earning him a playful smack on his chest.

"We figured why not plan a joint party, right where it all happened. Get ready to pack your bags, people. Wes is renting us an RV and we'll be hitting the road to Chicago."

"Really?" Ellie smiles as tears fill her eyes, as she stares up at Callum. Everyone knows what Ellie went through before she ended up boarding a bus to move here to Arbor Creek. Something tells me with the emotion on Callum's face, he's thinking about their road trip here that changed everything for him.

Kinsley rushes over to her, passing between where my eyes remain locked on Halle. Out of the corner of my eye, I see her wrap her arms around Ellie's shoulders. For the first time since I've returned home, I see the hurt in Halle's eyes.

It takes me a second before I connect the dots, but not only are we going back to where Callum and Ellie first met, but we're going to the place I took off to when I left Halle five years ago.

With her eyes on mine, she leans forward and snatches a shot of whiskey off the tray, as she raises it to me in cheers. Her eyebrow raises as the edge of her mouth covers up a sarcastic smile.

I hate the twist in my stomach, thinking about how much pain I caused her after I left. She tosses the shot back, slamming the glass down on the table. The burn stings her eyes, as the liquid lingers on her lips. Her tongue darts out, running along her lower lip, before she presses the back of her hand against her mouth.

The music surges through the speakers, drowning out everyone around us. The urge to close the distance between us and wrap my arms around her is strong. She must read my body language and the restraint I'm barely containing because she shakes her head no and it's like a splash of ice water over my head.

Halle has never pushed me away, not when she's hurting. Not even when there were times we were so heated from an argument, she'd never deny letting me hold her or touch her.

I can't blame her. I don't deserve her. I've pushed her away, left her here without any care to how ending us and taking off would hurt her. Watching her, she turns on her heel and takes off toward the bar. She makes it two steps before she disappears into the crowd.

"You okay?" Mason asks, I hadn't even realized he had gotten here. Brea's next to him with her arm wrapped around his.

"I'll go talk to her," Brea says, reassuringly.

"It'll be okay, man," Mason says, loud enough for only me to hear as he claps me on the back.

I wanted to believe him, I really did. The only thing I could think about though was the look on her face as she told me no.

As much as I've told myself to stay away from her, the thought of her feeling the same hits me harder than I ever expected. I'm starting to think things will never be okay with Halle and me again.

chapter seven

HALLE

"I'll have what she's having!" Brea shouts over the music, as she slides onto the barstool next to me.

"Hey." She smiles, bumping shoulders with me.

I look over at her, giving her the smile that matches the look I imagine I have on my face.

"Why so gloomy, pretty girl?"

"I just never expected it would be so hard to see him again. I've spent all this time wishing I could see him, wishing he were home. Now that he's here, I'm reminded of how much everything has changed between us. It almost makes me wish he weren't here again. At least I didn't have to worry about it being thrown in my face over and over, ya know?"

Things weren't always so easy for her and Mason. If there is anyone who can relate to how I'm feeling, it's her. Despite them being best friends before they started dating, there was a time when she felt like his past was thrown in her face too.

"Oh, I know alright," she says, as the bartender sets the shot glass in front of her and fills it with Jack Daniel's.

"I'll have another," I mutter. I need to call it quits after this one. Drowning my sorrows in liquor won't do me any good. If anything, it'll loosen the seal I have on my lips, which only gets me in trouble.

We toss them back together, as I slide the empty glass across the bar to where Danny stands.

"I understand why Kinsley planned this trip. It's perfect for Callum and Ellie, but I hate the idea of spending the weekend with Graham in the city he took off to when life got too hard for him. So hard he decided I wasn't worth the effort anymore, so he was going to throw in the towel on us too."

Getting it off my chest to someone feels good. Therapeutic almost. I've been putting on a smile for everyone around me. They have enough of their own shit. The last thing I need to do is burden them with my baggage from five years ago.

"It was hard enough thinking about who he was with and what he was doing when he was in Chicago. Now he's back here, looking like a damn G.I. Joe, throwing it in my face how sexy he looks. I can only imagine all the women he had throwing themselves at him."

Groaning, I rub my hand over my forehead. That last shot was probably not a good idea.

"Is that really what you're worried about?" she asks.

Rolling my head to the side, I see the smile she's working to cover. Narrowing my eyes at her, I imagine as if I'm shooting daggers at her right now.

"There's nothing funny about being sexually frustrated. Not all of us get to live with our smoking hot boyfriends, Brea. You have the freshly fucked glow about you, so don't look at me like you find my misery funny."

The smile falls from her face, knowing I just called her out. I throw my head back laughing.

"It wasn't like that, you know," she says, as my laughs stop.

I'm not sure if she's talking about her and Mason, or Graham.

"What do you mean?"

"Graham. It wasn't like that. Well, not entirely. There were women who noticed him, but it's hard not to."

Yeah, not at all what I wanted to hear.

"He wasn't interested. I never quite understood why he was so closed off and never giving them the time of day. Not until I met you."

Looking down at the solid oak of the bar, I clasp my hands together and twirl my thumbs in circles around each other.

"He meant everything to me. Everything. Until he wasn't anymore. Until he was gone, and he took my heart with him."

Tears fill my eyes, but I do my best to blink them away. Now is not the time to get all emotional. Not when he's standing ten feet away from me.

"Sorry," I mumble to Brea. "I just need to stop thinking about it."

"I understand," she says, running her arm over my shoulder, wrapping me in a side hug.

"I think this trip might actually be good for you. It's my old stomping grounds. I'm almost positive we will be hitting up Velvet, the nightclub we worked at."

Brea flashes the same smirk was wearing before, only this time I know she's up to something. She has this devious look on her face, like she's plotting something, and I want in on it.

"We will get all dressed up for the night out. It will be the perfect opportunity to remind him just what he's been missing."

Spinning on the barstool, I turn so I'm facing her. Glancing out onto the dance floor, my eyes wander over the crowd of people before they fall back on our group of friends. It doesn't take long before my eyes find Graham's.

Maybe it's the whiskey or maybe it's the feel of his eyes on me, but I can feel a warmth pass over me. His jaw is set, his face serious. He's rocking the perfect amount of facial hair and I can't help but remember how it felt against my skin.

I know he's wondering what we're talking about, but even more, he wants me to cool it on the drinking.

I want nothing more than to cross this bar and wrap my body around him. I don't want to wait until Chicago. I want to remind him of what he's been missing now.

Turning back to the bar, I wave Danny over and ask him to pour me a water.

"Geez, the tension between you two is enough to set this place on fire."

I want to laugh at my own misery again. It was always like that between us.

The level of passion we felt when we were together was so intense, it was scorching.

My face heats as the memories come flooding back, remembering the last night we were together.

Even after all this time, I still remember the look in his eyes as he picked me up, wrapping my legs around him. I loved the way he would grab my waist and hold me to him, tossing me around however he wanted.

I always felt safe in his arms. I knew Graham would never let anything happen to me.

The scent of his cologne hits me first, just as the heat of his body radiates at my back, forcing my back straight as I glance over my shoulder.

Danny sets a glass down in front of me, tossing some ice in along with it.

"You should slow down a little bit, don't you think?"

I knew he was watching me from across the bar, which is exactly why I wanted that second shot. It would drive him crazy, and that's exactly what I wanted.

"It's a good thing you don't have to worry about me anymore. Ain't that right, G?"

Throwing back the nickname our friends would use was like a smack in the face. I knew it, and I know he knew it too.

I never called him by his nickname in all our time together. Babe or handsome, yes. Never G.

"I'll give you two a minute," Brea says, as she slides off the barstool. She gives me a tense smile. I know without turning my head to face Graham that the comment did more than sting a little.

No, if I had to guess he's ready to toss me over his shoulder and march out of the building. Or at least, that's what the Graham I knew all those years ago would do.

I loved to push his buttons because I knew exactly how he would punish me for it.

Danny hits the button, filling the rest of the glass up with water. I know Graham is seeing this, too.

Taking a sip of water, it feels good as it slides down my throat. With the glass in hand, I turn back in my seat and focus my attention on him.

"Is it hot in here?" I ask, running the edge of the glass along the column of my neck. The sweat from the glass leaves a trail of water in its wake.

Graham's eyes follow the line of moisture from where it drips down my neck. I can feel his eyes blaze into me, as his body moves in closer bumping into where my legs sit crossed between us.

"Or is it just me?"

He presses in closer to me, urging me to uncross my legs and I do.

I come up to just below his chin from where I sit on the barstool.

Giving him access, he takes another step closer to me, but still holds himself back from touching me.

The heat, the tension radiating off us, causes my temperature to spike.

"I think it's just you," Graham says, running the palm of his hand from my knee up my thigh. Just the slightest bit of contact from him leaves my body eager, seeking out more from him.

The combination of his rough skin against mine causes goose pimples to rise over my skin, causing the muscles in my leg to shake.

"Graham," I sigh, my eyes closing as I tilt my head down, watching as his hand wraps around the side of my leg, gripping me tightly.

"Oh, I'm back to being Graham now?"

My eyes dart up to him, as his narrow at me.

I don't know what to say, as I hold the glass up to my mouth taking another drink. My tongue darts out, running along the edge of my lip.

It's starting to get to him, his chest heaves with every forced breath he takes.

He mutters something about me being a pain in the ass as he releases his grip on my thigh, running it over his face.

"Promise me you won't try to drive home tonight."

That was not at all what I expected him to say, especially given the way he was just looking at me. His reaction to our close proximity.

I'm not sure if I'm more surprised or hurt. By the look on his face staring back at me, I'm guessing he's picking up on it too.

"Will you let me take you home?"

"Awfully forward of you, don't you think? Just assuming after all this time, I'd let you take me home."

The thought of him coming home with me tonight leaves my mouth dry with want. Even thinking about it now makes me feel desperate to say yes. More than him just driving me home, I want more time with him. More of having him close.

Even if it won't lead to the more that I am hoping for, I can't help but want anything with Graham.

When Graham left five years ago, to say I was a wreck would be an understatement. We'd have our share of arguments, what couple doesn't though, right?

I knew this was different though. I knew when Graham told me he was leaving, there was going to be no going back. I think there was a part of me that thought, or maybe hoped is the better word, he would realize he was wrong and made the biggest mistake of his life. No matter what life threw at us, we'd weather the storm together.

With each day that passed where I didn't hear from him, it was another reminder that the future I hoped for us grew further and further away.

Him being here now, having the chance to be near him again, despite knowing he could hurt me again, I want to say yes. I want to give in and soak up whatever I time I have with him.

Which is exactly why I don't.

"I'm fully capable of making sure I get home on my own. I've been doing it for the past five years without your concern. You don't have to take care of me, G."

There's a subtle tic in his jaw and I know I've succeeded at getting under his skin.

Sliding off the barstool, I put my feet on the floor. He doesn't move to take a step back, but his eyes follow mine as I step in closer to him.

I stare up at him, feeling the warmth of his body and the feel of his breath feather over my cheek. I want to reach up and pull him close to me, to press my lips against his again. I want to know if he tastes as good as I remember.

I move to step around him, but before I'm able to get far, his hand wraps around the span of my hip.

"Halle," he breathes, leaning in closer to me.

It's loud in here, but I swear over the sound of the music I can hear my heart beating. I wonder for a moment if he can hear it too.

"I'm sorry," he whispers.

I close my eyes and try to gain some semblance of control, trying to avoid the tears forming in my eyes and once again hoping they don't fall.

"I know I hurt you." His voice breaks, as he lets out a deep breath. Neither of us move though. Neither of us try to break this connection between us. "I understand you're still angry. I deserve it. I deserve for you to be angry with me. I just hope you know I'd give anything to take your pain away. I'm so damn sorry."

With that, he turns and walks back to where our friends stand on the other side of the bar. His movements are confident, which are nothing like how I am feeling right now.

No, I feel like I'm on the edge of crumbling.

As much as I want to stay here, to celebrate Ellie and Callum with the rest of my friends, I just want to leave. I want to go home, nurse my wounds, and prepare to spend the weekend with our friends in Chicago.

But I don't. Instead, I muster up every bit of strength I have in me, I follow along behind him to our friends. I'll lick my wounds in peace tomorrow, with a pint of Ben and Jerry's and a glass of rosé.

Tonight, I'm going to forget the ache in my heart I've carried for Graham Shaw and focus on being there for my friends.

chapter eight

GRAHAM

I know I shouldn't let her get to me the way she does, but I can't help it. I've never been able to control the emotions she evokes in me, even after all these years.

The rest of the night goes by painfully slow. Halle spends most of the night laughing with the girls, while I try to do my best to keep my eyes off her. I thought after my apology, maybe it would ease the tension between us, but it seems like it's only done the opposite.

She doesn't look my way for the rest of the night.

A little while later, after I step away to use the restroom, I feel the pang in my chest when I return to find Halle missing.

"Halle left," Kinsley says, as if picking up on my question. "She told us to tell you goodbye."

She gives me a forced smile. Deciding to call it a night, too, I make my way around the table saying goodbye to my friends. Callum and Ellie are wrapped around each other on the dance floor. I don't want to ruin their moment, so I ask Mason to tell his brother bye for me and I'll see them next weekend when we take the trip to Chicago.

Kinsley stops me before I can make a beeline out the door.

"G, I don't know what's going on between you two. She won't talk to me about it, but I know she's torn apart seeing you again. She may not say it, but I know she's thinking about how things used to be."

I think about it too. When I was eighteen years old, she was everything to me. She was all I could see. She was like a ray of sunshine into my life. I would've done anything for her.

I will continue to do anything for her to make her happy. I don't deserve her, her light, her goodness. I don't deserve Halle, I never have.

"Nothing's going on between us. I just wanted to make sure she got home okay."

Kinsley's laugh pulls my attention away from where my eyes are focused on the door, where she went. It's loud and full, nearly causing her to fold her body in half letting it out.

"What's so funny?"

"You! You're so clueless. Nothing is going on? Are you serious?"

I want to say "yes, I'm serious" but she's right. I'm a fool if I think we could be in the same town and know nothing would happen between us.

"I don't deserve her, Kins. I don't. Everything's so fucked up."

"You do deserve each other. Just promise me you won't hurt her again or so help me, Graham Shaw," she sighs, pointing her two fingers at her eyes and back to me. She squints her eyes, trying to intimidate me.

"I never wanted to hurt her. I'd rather rip my own heart out than do anything to hurt her. Please tell me you know that."

Kinsley drops her hand, as the sadness returns to her face. Leaving Arbor Creek was never about wanting to hurt her but protecting her from me. She made me do reckless things to be near her and I'd never want the recklessness to lead to her being hurt.

Saying goodbye to Kinsley, I wave to my friends before heading toward the back door I entered through earlier that night. Stepping outside, I'm hit with the cool breeze. The sun has long since gone down and the heat from earlier in the day has settled into a cool air without the sunshine beating down on me.

Walking across the parking lot, the sound of the gravel crunches beneath my feet as I hit the lock on my truck. The sound of the alarm beeps, just as I hear the soft whimpers in the distance.

"It's okay, Halle. It's okay." I hear whispered, causing my entire body to tense.

The sound of her muffled words has me on high alert, searching around me for the source of her cries.

"Halle, is that you?" My voice is firm, loud.

"Graham?" she asks. Her eyes blink beneath the dim light in the parking lot. They are full, with tears streaming down her face.

I want to stop and just stare in awe at her beauty, but I remind myself she has been crying. Despite what I just got done telling Kinsley, nothing is going on and I would never hurt her; I can't deny whatever is hurting her now I want to be the one to be there for her. I want to be the one who holds her, comforts her.

Jogging across the parking lot, I approach her and pull her car door open. Crouching down next to her, I put my hand on her knee.

"What's wrong?"

Her eyes are cast downward, taking in my hand wrapped around her knee.

"What have you been getting into?" she asks, her voice quivering, lighting a match inside me. It's like a switch flipped from good to evil. "Graham, what did you do?"

The sound of an ignition starting pulls me away from her, to the loud engine behind us. As soon as my eyes fall on the source, I feel the ice fill my veins. I'm torn between wanting to cross the parking lot and lay him out and wanting to wrap my arm around Halle and get her out of here.

I'm kicking myself for letting her walk out here by herself. My mind drifts back to the conversation I had earlier this week, the information that had come in from an informant about how they had spotted Krate in the parking lot of Brodie's.

Seeing the black GTO parked behind her, I stand to full height not shying away from the coward who I know is behind the wheel. Whatever happened has everything to do with me and this bastard.

All I see is red. I want nothing more than to pull him out of the car and rip him to shreds. The lights flash in front of my eyes, as he puts the car into reverse and slowly backs out of the parking spot.

As the car turns, pulling out, his eyes meet mine.

"Oh, God," Halle mutters to herself. "Graham, stop! Don't go," she cries, reading my mind.

Flexing my jaw, I stare him down, sending a message to him not to fuck with me, but the smile that lines his mouth has me curling my hand into a fist as he hits the gas and peels out of the parking lot. When his car turns the corner, pulling out of the lot, I'm next to Halle in an instant.

"C'mon, I'm going to give you a ride home. You can tell me what happened in the car. I want to make sure you get home safe. I'll have Maverick come by tomorrow and drive your car to the salon."

Holding my hand out to her, she puts hers in mine as I help her out of the car. I don't move to let go until we approach my pickup and I help her into the cab.

We drive in silence the two minutes it takes to get to her place. Pulling up alongside of her apartment building, I put the gear in park and roll my head to the side to glance over at Halle.

"Tell me what happened, Hals."

The light from the dashboard casts a soft glow on her face, giving me just enough to see the sweet curve of her smile. I know she likes hearing me call her by the same nickname I had for her all those years ago.

"It was nothing at first. He was just hitting on me, acting like he wanted to take me home. But then he." She pauses, glancing back over at me. "He asked where you were. Said he couldn't believe you let me out of your sight long enough for him to talk to me."

My grip on the steering wheel tightens.

"Has he pulled this shit before?"

The anger is rising in my voice, taking her off guard. Normally I can keep my temper in check. I'm not usually one to fly off the handle like this, especially not around her.

Something about knowing this skeevy fucker is trying to get close to my Halle pisses me off.

Her eyes narrow at me as she lets out a heavy sigh. She doesn't know what I know though. She doesn't realize how tangled up into my past, into what happened to Gage, we believe he is. I can't tell her, at least not yet, but dammit I want to. I want her to know so she understands and so she'll stay the fuck away from him.

"Listen, Graham," she says, but I hold my hand up stopping her.

"Don't go there with me, Halle. This isn't one of those topics you can fire back at me about how I don't need to worry about you and you can do whatever the hell you want. Not about this, not with you. Whether you like it or not, I'm gonna worry about you. If it's you, it is my damn business. Let me make this clear, we will not be goin' there. Not ever."

Halle lets out a heavy sigh, as she crosses her arms over her stomach. I watch as she runs her finger over her thumbnail, before she glances up meeting my eyes.

"I'm going to ask you again, Halle; has he tried to pull this shit before?"

She presses her lips into a thin line, contemplating, before she finally answers.

"No, he hasn't. I don't know why, but I have a feeling he was only doing it because of you."

She doesn't know why but hearing her say it I know she's not wrong.

"Why do you say that?"

"I saw him poking around your truck before I got outside. I think I caught him off guard when he saw me coming." Her eyebrows furrow as she looks at me. "I'm not sure what he would be looking for. You've never been one to keep your vehicles very clean."

She looks down at the floor, kicking her foot at the sweatshirt and empty bottle of motor oil sitting on the floor. I've been meaning to throw it away, I just haven't got around to it.

"Just do me a favor, Hals. Please just stay away from Krate and any of the scumbags he runs around with, alright? They're not good people, and I don't trust them," I say, lowering my voice. I know she can hear the worry in my voice as she peers up at me.

She's trying to get a read on me, figure out what I'm not telling her but doesn't fight me for more answers. I'm grateful as hell for it too. I don't want to lie to her, but now isn't the time that I fill her in on this. Not yet anyway.

"Okay," she says. Very rarely does she give into me without pushing.

"You may not believe me. I certainly don't deserve your trust anymore, but I don't know what I'd do if anything ever happened to you."

My mind filters back to the night Gage died, the panic that consumed me. Picturing being in that moment but with Halle on the other end, I just can't.

Resting my chin on my closed fist, I glance out the window at the street light in the alley behind her apartment building. The light is about to go out, so it flashes every few seconds. I let it distract me from the darkness of my thoughts.

"I do," she whispers, catching me off guard. My eyebrows furrow and for a second, I'm unsure of what she's talking about, but then my comment comes back to me. Hearing her tell me, even after everything happened and the pain I put her through, she still trusts me carries a lot of weight.

Her hand reaches across the center console and brushes against my bicep. My arm flexes under her touch. I can feel the warmth of the contact radiating down my arm and throughout my body. Only she has ever been able to make me feel this way. Seeing her, touching her tonight for the first time in years, it makes me wonder what I was thinking letting her go and leaving her behind.

I have thought about her every day for the past five years. When I first left, she would call or text me almost every day. For the longest time, I would sit and replay the voice mails she would leave, just using the sound of her voice as a connection to the loss I felt aching in my stomach. I saved her text messages and would re-read them when I was thinking about her, regretting my decision to leave. I left her with nothing but a goodbye, yet I used her words telling me she missed me to get through every day.

It made me feel incredibly selfish but giving her the same in return would've only been to ease the guilt I felt inside. It wasn't going to help her move on, so every time I thought about responding back, I closed the message and turned off my phone.

When the messages stopped, I told myself I had lost her. She had let me go and I deserved to lose her. I hurt her in unmeasurable ways and I didn't deserve the way she continued to put herself out there, not wanting to let me go. I thought she had and maybe I still have lost her, but hearing her say she still trusts me, even when I know I don't deserve it, means more to me than I could ever put into words.

Reaching up, my hand folds over hers. Holding her small hand out in front of me, I press a soft kiss against the palm of her hand. I hear her breath hitch, not expecting the move, but I don't let it stop me as I kiss down her palm to her wrist as her hand presses against my cheek.

For a moment, I close my eyes and soak in the feeling of her hand again in the same way I held onto her words. We sit like this for a few minutes. No sound, no words. Just the peace of having her next to me again filling the silence between us.

When I finally work up the courage to open my eyes, I'm surprised when I see the tears filling the brim of her eye.

"Halle," I say, turning in my seat to face her. I hate seeing her cry. It physically pains me to see her anything but happy.

"No, it's okay." She waves me off, as she runs her finger underneath the edge of her eye, avoiding eye contact with me.

"I should head inside. It's been a long day and I'm exhausted," she says, looking back at me. She puts a smile on, but I know better than to believe it. It doesn't meet her eyes and I know she's just forcing it, doing her best to fight off the urge to show any emotions.

I want to push her on it. I want to beg her to stay here, with me. I want to change the subject and promise her it will be different, but I can also see the fatigue in her eyes. The exhaustion that's weighing on her, so I decide against it.

It's not the time or place. I don't deserve for her to give me a second more of her time, even if I'm a selfish, greedy bastard who wants to soak up her sun and bask in it.

"Alright," I say, sitting forward to turn off the ignition.

"You don't have to get out. I can see myself inside. Thank you for the ride and making sure I was okay."

"Of course," I say, reluctantly.

The edge of her mouth curves into a small smile as she reaches forward to grab her purse, pulling the keys out and clutches them in her hand.

She mutters out a soft "goodnight" as she slips out of the passenger seat and shuts the door behind her. As soon as she's gone, I feel like all the air is sucked out of me and I'm left feeling deflated.

I watch her toned legs eat up the distance, taking her further away from me. My eyes don't leave her as she climbs up the stairs. She turns back to see if I'm still here and when she spots me watching her, she raises her hand in a small wave before sticking the key in her door and disappearing inside.

It hits me how much things have changed between us over the years. I hate how different this feels. This isn't who we are, how things were supposed to be. Regardless, I know there is no one to blame for this but myself.

Turning the key in the ignition, I shift the gear into drive and head for home. I force myself to remember why I made the decisions I have, and, in the end, I know Halle is better off without me.

For those few minutes though, I let myself wish it were different.

chapter nine

HALLE

Clicking the turn signal, I pull onto the gravel road that winds down to Callum and Ellie's house. Wes got an RV for us to drive to Chicago where we'll spend the weekend celebrating their upcoming wedding.

I've spent the last two weeks thinking about this trip. On one hand, I'm thrilled to spend the weekend with my friends, but then on the other, I've been lost in thought about what it will be like to be in Chicago. In the city Graham escaped to when life got to be too tough.

When he gave up on us and decided I wasn't worth it anymore.

Callum and Ellie originally met when they were boarding a bus, traveling back home from Chicago. Callum had spent the weekend visiting his brother, Mason, and was coming back home to Arbor Creek.

Ellie grew up living in a small town, Garwood, outside of Chicago. Ellie didn't have it easy. She boarded a bus, moving to Arbor Creek, and moved into a house Kinsley's grandfather was renting out at the time. We've heard the story countless times of how she was boarding the bus and fell into Callum. He loves to talk about how he swept her off her feet.

Pulling up in front of their house, their driveway is bustling with people. Mason and Brea are here, unloading his truck with their bags. Brannon and Dean are standing in the front yard, laughing about something. I hadn't expected to see Dean here, considering he lives in Chicago, but he must've been visiting.

Parking next to Mason, I check my appearance in the rearview mirror. I was fully expecting to see Graham here, but by the looks of things, he's not here. There's a small knot in my stomach forming at the thought of him not coming this weekend.

That thought is quickly pushed out of my mind when I hear the deep rumble of a pickup truck pull up beside me.

Glancing over, my heart starts to come back to life as I take in the profile of his handsome face. He's wearing aviator sunglasses and a black fitted T-shirt.

"Damn it," I mutter to myself.

I've gone to war in my head over the thought of going to Chicago. I hate everything about big cities and the thought of going here leaves me frustrated. Looking at him and how delicious he looks, I am even more frustrated. Not just the sexual kind.

"You can do this, Halle. You have a plan and you're going to execute it to perfection."

Turning back to the rearview mirror, I untwist the cap to my lip gloss and expertly apply the shimmer over my lips before rubbing them together. Fixing a few strands of my hair, I slide the lip gloss back into my purse and push open the door.

The last two times Graham and I have been around each other, I could tell how hard it is for him to stay away from me. There's a familiarity there between us. Even though he's fighting against it, I can see he's struggling to keep his distance.

The plan for this weekend is to remind him of what he let go of when he left me. I want to drive him so crazy he lets go of the control he's been holding onto and gives into what I know he's been missing.

As soon as I step out of the car, I spot Brea over the hood of my car. Her long brown hair is wrapped in a messy bun sitting on the top of her head. Her eyes always stand out like crystals with her long eyelashes.

I pop the trunk and begin pulling out my suitcase.

"You need any help?" Brea asks, her voice full of excitement.

Once she's standing close enough to me, her voice drops down low enough so only I can hear her. "You're doing it, aren't you? Hals, you're dressed to fucking kill right now. When he sees your legs, he's going to be falling all over himself."

Brea chuckles, her laughs start carrying on. "I can just picture him now. Oh, God, this is going to be good."

"You're damn fucking right I'm doing it." I smile, wiggling my eyebrows up and down. "He thought he could come back to town lookin' like a fucking snack and thought I wasn't going to want some. Try again. I'm not going to be the one to give in though. Nope," I say with the pop. "Not happening. He walked away and gave up on me. It'll be him who will be crawling back to me, not the other way around."

"Damn straight." Brea laughs.

The sound of honking behind us has us both turning our heads over our shoulders to see who it is, when we spot Wes pulling up the driveaway. Kinsley is sitting next to him, hitting the horn as she waves enthusiastically.

"She lives for this, doesn't she?"

"Oh, God, yes!" I giggle.

Hoisting my suitcase out of my trunk, I set it on the ground as I see Graham and his large frame out of my peripheral. My knees get a little weak just being near him, but I force myself to get it together.

Giving in, I glance over at him, and I feel like I could come on the spot at the way his arm flexes holding his gym bag in his hand. Rubbing my lips together again, I drink in his tan skin over his broad chest to his handsome face. His light brown hair almost looks underneath the sunlight.

I hate that he's wearing sunglasses. I wish I could read the look on his face when he sees me.

"Hey," he croaks.

Hearing the crack in his voice causes sweat to break out over my skin. It's already warm outside, with the humidity the weatherman said it would get close to ninety degrees today. The heat I feel rushing through me isn't just from the warm temperatures, but everything to do with having his eyes on me once again.

"Here we go again." Brea giggles from behind me, causing a grin to spread out over my face.

"Hey, Graham." I smile.

His eyes rake over my body, before meeting my eyes. I swear for a minute I hear him mutter "shit," but I can't be sure if it was him or a voice in the distance.

"Want me to help you with that?" he asks, pointing to my suitcase, sounding more confident this time.

Looking down at my suitcase and back up to him, I tell him thank you as he steps closer to me. He smells so good and it reminds me how hard having him around this weekend is going to be.

He smells clean, like fresh linen, and something else that's uniquely Graham. It's hypnotizing and arousing, all at the same time.

"It's good to see you, sunshine. You look good."

The mention of my nickname causes my heart to drop. I force a smile on my face to hide the way it hits me hearing him call me sunshine again.

I want so badly to wrap my arms around him and melt into his body, the way I always would when he called me his sunshine.

"You do too," I mutter. "You happy to be going back to Chicago?"

As soon as the words leave my mouth, I realize how nervous I am to hear the answer. I almost wish I could press rewind and take it all back.

Lifting his arm, he runs his hand through his hair looking somewhere behind me, before he looks back down at me.

"Not as happy as I am to be home."

The way he says home eases some of the restraints I had around my heart, making it easier to breathe easier again.

"Good." I smile. "We're glad to have you home."

We're loaded up and on the road by ten in the morning. The RV Wes was able to get for us is beautiful. It has so much room, which is good considering we have five guys and four girls along for the trip, we need it. We have a long drive ahead of us, so I park it at the table with the girls. The guys took over the living area, watching ESPN highlights on the TV.

"Are you guys going to tell me what we have planned for tonight?" Ellie asks, her eyes bouncing to each of us for any sign of who's going to spill it.

Ellie's the most low-key out of all of us. She's not much of a partier, so I'm sure she's wondering what the heck we have in store for her when we get there.

The truth is, I don't have the slightest idea what Kinsley has up her sleeve. She's been tight-lipped about everything.

"Do you trust me?" Kinsley asks, a devious smile on her face.

"I do..." Ellie says slowly, her eyes narrowing at Kinsley. "Although I'm starting to wonder how much I should be trusting you.

"Please tell me you didn't do anything crazy like get strippers or something," Ellie says hesitantly. Her eyes glance to Callum, who's sitting behind Kinsley, making sure he didn't hear her before shooting back to Kinsley.

Kinsley barks out a laugh and I can't help but chuckle at the comment. Callum would lose his shit if Kinsley had her near a guy, much less shirtless.

I almost wish she would because it'd be entertaining to see.

"Are you serious?" Kinsley asks, deadpanned. "I'm not trying to ruin our trip here, Ellie. We both know Callum wouldn't like the idea. At all."

"I wouldn't like what?" Callum asks, silencing everyone.

Everyone except me, of course.

"Oh, we were just saying you wouldn't mind if we stole Ellie for the night. Took her out to the strip club, let her experience her last night as a single woman. You know, make sure she's sowed all her wild oats before she's a one-man woman for the rest of her life."

I grin, knowing exactly the reaction I'm getting from him.

Callum growls, shooting a look over at Kinsley before looking back at me. He's trying to tell if I'm joking or serious.

"C'mon, Callum, let her live a little." I giggle, winking at him.

Glancing over at Graham, I bite my lip when I see the grin on his face. He shakes his head when his eyes connect with mine, seeing through me, knowing I'm pushing his buttons.

"I don't think so," Callum says, serious. His words are firm, unwavering. "I won't share her. Not with anyone."

His eyes look to Ellie. "Ever," he says, punctuating the end.

Ellie slides out from where she's seated in the booth to where Callum sits on the other side of the walkway, sitting on his lap. His arms are around her waist, holding her to him in a move that's both possessive and protective.

Callum's feathers can be easily ruffled, especially where Ellie is concerned. He knows damn good and well not only would we never disrespect him, but she'd never agree to it anyway.

It's still fun to see how uptight he can be when we talk about it.

I find myself staring at the way he runs his hands up and down her leg as the other is wrapped in her hair. He takes her in a deep kiss, and I immediately look away, feeling like I'm eavesdropping on their private moment.

I'm surprised when I see Graham's eyes looking back at me. He glances over at Callum and Ellie, before looking back to me again.

I'm jealous of Callum and Ellie's love. They've been through a lot, but he would do anything for her. He'd take on the world to protect her. She's his world.

I wonder if Graham is thinking about the same things I am. How seeing them together reminds me so much of us and the way things used to be when we were together.

The possessive nature in which Callum wraps his fingers in Ellie's hair, kissing her with so much passion, you feel like if you stand too close, you'll sense the light flicks of the fire snapping from them and soon you'll be engulfed in the same flames.

For a moment, I picture myself sitting in Graham's lap, his arms banded around me, holding me against him as I wrap my arms around his neck. We hold each other with so much force, we leave little room between us.

I can almost feel his breath feather over my skin, as our bodies rock against one another. My eyes flutter closed as I imagine his lips on mine and his tongue seeking entrance into my mouth. His moan hitting my ears the moment our tongues connect.

"Halle," Kinsley cuts through my thoughts.

Her eyes are wide and for a moment I start to wonder if the moan I heard was in my thoughts and didn't come from me.

My eyes fall on Kinsley's as heat spreads over my face, as the wetness floods in me. "Are you okay?"

"Yeah, I'm fine," I say, sliding out of the seat. My legs feel like jelly, as I test my balance. "I just need to use the restroom." Looking down the hall, I look back to her and force a smile.

Racing down the hallway, I slip into the bathroom. Slamming the door shut behind me, I hit the lock before I collapse onto the closed lid.

"What the fuck?" I groan into my hands, feeling mortified. "What the hell is wrong with me?"

I seriously about orgasmed at a table in front of all my friends, just thinking about my ex-boyfriend putting his hands on me again. My ex who is sitting two feet away from me, much less.

I need to get my shit together and quick if I'm sticking to the plan.

I actually consider unbuttoning my pants and taking care of business myself, when there's a light knock on the door, causing me to freeze.

"You alright in there?" Graham's deep voice rumbles through the door. Each word vibrates through my body, as I squeeze my thighs together needing some friction between my legs.

Forcing out a deep breath, I stand and take in my appearance in the mirror. Am I alright? Holy shit, I don't look alright. I look like a cat about to pounce.

"Yeah," I say. Running my fingers through my hair, I pull on the front of my T-shirt to get a little air flow moving. I am so turned on, I feel like my body is overheating. "Just give me a sec."

Turning on the water in the sink, I run the cool water over my hands before patting my cheeks trying to cool down my skin. I force myself to think of things, like the taste of black licorice and the smell of microwaved cauliflower, and just like that all the thoughts I had earlier evaporate from my mind.

Well, that is until I slide the bathroom door open and come face to face with the man who makes me think so many dirty thoughts, it should be considered illegal.

"Everything okay?"

Guessing by the look on his face, he knows exactly how not okay I'm feeling.

My eyes narrow at the comment and I want to tell him to just shut up. To close your mouth and not talk for the rest of the trip so I don't have to listen to your ridiculously sexy voice.

No, I'm not okay. I'm the furthest thing from okay. I'm coming out of my skin right now, that's how not okay I am.

He looks at me, his eyes looking down at my lips as I rub them together, before looking me straight in the eyes again.

"You need help with anything?"

For a moment I think he's serious, but then his lip curls up at the edge in a smile, and I realize he's fucking with me. He knows he's getting under my skin now and he's messing with me, thinking it's funny.

That's where he's wrong, you see, because I have a plan. Forcing a smile on my face, I look up at him and grin.

Reaching out, I grab the front of Graham's shirt and pull him closer to me. It's a bold move, especially considering how close I'm treading to the brink of giving into him right now.

"That's real sweet of you, Graham." I look up at him, giving him a coy smile. "But I took care of it."

I flash him a wink before stepping around him, walking back down the hallway and taking a seat at the table.

Point 1 for me.

chapter ten

GRAHAM

She's killing me. Fucking killing me.

My eyes drink in their fill of her as she walks down the hallway like her ass is on fire.

Her legs. Fuck me, those legs. They've been the focal point of many of my fantasies. The look in her eyes, I knew that look. I remember what she looks like when she's about to fall apart before me. I've memorized it and engraved it into my memory.

Reaching down, I adjust my aching cock in my pants.

I spend the rest of the trip doing my best to avoid Halle. I don't even look her way. It's early evening by the time we arrive in Chicago and check into the hotel. You'd think we'd all be tired from the traveling, but it's the exact opposite. I'm just ready to get out and stretch my legs.

We opt to stay at the Westin hotel located downtown. Kinsley insisted on it since it's the hotel where Callum stayed at when he was visiting Chicago the day he met Ellie. It's also near Velvet. I haven't been back here since before I moved.

After we check in, we decide to head up to our rooms with the plan to meet back down in the lobby in an hour to head to dinner. We all crowd into the elevator, making our way to our rooms.

Everyone here is coupled off, except for Halle and Brannon, so I decided to get my own room. The last thing I wanted to worry about was waking up in the middle of the night hearing shit I have no business hearin'.

As the elevator climbs higher and higher, everyone slowly exits the elevator and before too long it's just Halle and me alone together once again.

Leaning against the back wall, I look forward with my eyes fixed on Halle in the mirror in front of us. I know she is aware of my eyes on her, as she stares up at the monitor reading the floors as we make our way to the eighth floor.

The elevator dings as we make our arrival and, once again, she's out of the door like the devil is hot on her heels. With my bag in my hand, I follow along right behind her and am surprised when I see her stop at Room 827.

The odds are working in my favor apparently, as I move to stand next to her, holding my keycard in front of the scanner to Room 825.

"See you at dinner, Halle," I say, just as the green light flashes and I open the door.

She mutters out a response, before she quickly scurries inside and the door slams behind her.

The entire time I'm in the shower, my mind is back on her. I picture her in the room next door, crawling up onto the bed. I think about her slipping those shorts over her hips and down her sexy as fuck legs, before her hand slides down between them, rubbing her fingers over her clit.

I imagine her thinking about me, pretending it's me who's touching her, my mouth that's between her legs, up her stomach, before my lips wrap around her nipple. The thought of her shuttered breaths as she lets out a quiet moan forces me to squeeze my dick so hard, I worry the damage I could do, as cum shoots out onto the tile of the shower wall.

Pressing my arm against the wall, I let the steady stream of water fall against my back as I struggle to gather my breath and not collapse on the floor.

Pulling myself together, I finish washing up in the shower before stepping out and drying off with the towel. As much as I hate to admit it, I feel a lot better.

The weather in Chicago is warm, despite the cool breeze at night whipping through the windy city. I go for more of a casual look, dressed in my dark denim jeans, boots, and heathered button up shirt.

Checking the time, I pause for any sign that maybe Halle is next door and I consider waiting until I hear her door opening and closing before I head down to the lobby. Deciding against it though, I quickly put on deodorant and cologne and head down to meet my friends.

I don't see Halle there, so I was right. She's still getting ready. I picture her standing in the bathroom with her hair and makeup products littering the counter, music playing on her phone while she gets ready.

She used to always make the biggest mess when she would get ready. I would always ask her what she needed all that shit for when she was naturally beautiful. She didn't need a damn thing on her face to look pretty. She'd just roll her eyes at me, tell me to be quiet, as she'd pick up her brush using it as a microphone to sing whatever song was playing at the time.

Brannon, Wes, and Kinsley are all gathered around in the lobby. Kinsley's scrolling through her phone, while absent-mindedly talking to Wes about the itinerary for the evening. I don't bother worrying about what she has planned. I trust she has it all taken care of. I don't need to get in her way, she'll make sure I am where I'm supposed to be.

While we wait for the rest of the crew to meet up with us, Brannon and I talk about the upcoming Iowa football season until Callum, Ellie, Mason, and Brea join us a few minutes later.

"Dammit, Halle. Of course, you have to be the last one to arrive," Kinsley huffs.

I want to laugh at Kinsley. It drives her crazy when Halle is late.

Glancing over at the bank of elevators, I consider asking her if she wants me to run upstairs quick when Halle steps out of the elevator. Her long blonde hair is curled in waves, pulled over her shoulder. She's dressed in a black fitted dress. The straps are small, only about an inch wide. As she comes closer to me, I admire the lace material that covers her body. Staring at her, I watch the subtle bob of her throat as she swallows, and it takes everything in me not to pull her in my arms and kiss up her neck, feeling the lace beneath my fingers.

She looks fucking stunning. A knock-out.

Drinking in every inch of her body, I follow the path down to her legs to the black heels strapped around her ankles. If I had half a mind, I'd haul her over my shoulder and carry her ass back upstairs to my room. The last thing I want is anyone else drinking their fill of her in that dress.

I picture the looks she'll get tonight, and I can't help the possessiveness in me. I want to keep her for me and my eyes only.

"Damn," Brannon mutters, as I shoot him a look before turning to stare at Halle once more.

"Hi, boys," Halle says, flashing me a wink before looking over at Brannon.

"Pick your jaw up off the floor, Brannon. It's not a good look for you." Halle laughs, as she struts over to where Brea and Ellie are standing.

"She sure does have a mouth on her," Brannon retorts.

Growling, he looks over at me and laughs again. "Easy. I'm just making observations. To be fair, you're the one who put her back on the market."

I want to tell him to fuck off, but I'm too distracted by Halle's legs in this lace dress to care. She looks incredible and I know without even asking, she wore this dress tonight knowing she'd be seeing me.

She's tempting me, and she knows just the way to bring me to my knees.

Callum clears his throat and everyone turns their attention to him.

"Kinsley, I owe you for this. You all look amazing tonight," Callum says, as the rest of the guys nod our heads in agreement. Callum laces his fingers with Ellie, raising them to his lips. "Ellie, baby, you look absolutely beautiful. I can't wait to make you mine forever."

Ellie's cheeks flush a rosy pink as Callum kisses her.

"I'm going to be honest with you though, Kinsley. If you don't get this show on the road, I'm going to take my soon-to-be wife upstairs and you won't see either of us until it's time to head home."

Ellie laughs, smacking him on his chest, as he wraps his arms around her pulling her into a kiss.

"Alright, you two," Kinsley reprimands. "You can hang out with us for a little bit and then you can go do whatever you want to do. I have plans tonight and I'm not going to let you ruin them."

Before Callum and Ellie can think about escaping back upstairs to their suite, Kinsley has us all out the door and into an Uber. We go out to dinner at a nice restaurant not too far from the hotel called Glass Glow, before we're dropped off outside of Velvet.

"Oh my God," Brea sighs, wrapping her arm around Mason's as she smiles up at him. "This brings back so many memories. I miss it here."

It really does. We've had so many great memories working together at Velvet. It's hard to believe it's only been a few months since we were living in Chicago.

Glancing over at Halle, her eyes are fixed on me. They have this far out look about them and, for a moment, I wonder what she's thinking about. She had to have heard what Brea said and I feel like an idiot for not thinking about what being here would do to her.

She gives me a forced smile and my eyes narrow, before I smile back.

The sky is dark, but the lights of downtown Chicago make it feel just as bright as if it were the middle of the afternoon. Although with the sun having set, the heat has cooled down making the windy city feel brisker.

We move to stand in line just before I hear the loud bark of my name, and I turn to see Craig standing there. He's the owner of Velvet and, honestly, is more like a father to me.

He waves at me, before waving me over to him. When he sees just me coming, he shouts, "All of you, c'mon."

I hear Kinsley joke about how it pays to have connections, as I walk over to the man that has played such a huge role in my life.

"It's good to see you, Son." He smiles, looking behind me over to Mason and Brea. Brea wraps her arms around him, telling him it's good to see him just before Mason claps him on the back saying the same.

We bypass the line of people waiting to enter, walking into the front of Velvet. Glancing behind me, I check that my friends are following along behind me. Kinsley and Halle both have this wide-eyed look about them. When you grow up in Arbor Creek and the extent of your clubbing is Friday nights at Brodie's, it's a little more of a culture shock. I don't think they quite knew what they'd be getting themselves into tonight.

Before we're even two steps inside, I hear one of the bartenders and Brea's former roommate, Lissa, cheering excitedly when she sees Brea and Mason. She ushers everyone over to the tables reserved along the side of the bar, while I hang back taking a few minutes to catch up with Craig.

"How are you doing, Son? How's the business going?"

"Things are going well. My mom is doing well. You know how hard it was for me to think about going back to Iowa, but honestly..." I sigh, looking over at Halle and my friends, as Lissa has her notepad out taking their drink orders. "Honestly, it's really good to be back home. I know for the longest time I said I'd never go back, and I really believed it. I have good friends though and they really are helping make it easier."

"I'm so glad to hear it," Craig says, clapping me on the shoulder. "I'm really proud of you, you know? You're doing such great things for yourself."

Turning to look at Craig, I detect the glint of happiness in his eye and I know he really means it.

"Which one is she?" he asks, taking me completely off guard. I know without asking him to elaborate who he's referring to. "Wait, don't tell me, let me guess."

I laugh, seeing the wide smile on his face.

"She's the blonde one in the black dress, right?"

It really can't be too hard to figure it out. He already knows who Brea is, so that's off the table. There is Ellie, who is standing next to Callum who has his arm permanently glued to her side. Then, there's Kinsley who's running through the bachelor/bachelorette party games with Halle seated, looking somewhat relaxed as she laughs with Brannon about something. I grit my teeth watching as Halle brushes her hand against Brannon's arm, as her eyes flash over to mine. She knows I'm watching her and her obvious display of flirting with my friend.

The sound of glass shattering at the bar next to us has both Craig and I turning our attention to where Lissa is rounding up the order of drinks. Lissa raises her hand to her mouth as she mutters "ouch" repeatedly, spurring Craig and me into action.

"Are you okay?" I mutter, helping clean up the spilled vodka on the bar being careful as I pick up the shards of glass.

"Just great," she responds. There is a hint of annoyance in her voice.

"You sure about that?" I ask, raising my eyebrow at her not buying it at all.

"Are they, like, together?"

She motions with her head over to the table and it dawns on me that she's asking about Brannon and Halle. I'm surprised she asks, honestly. The first time she met Brannon was when she was dating her ex-boyfriend, Adam, and he didn't shy away from hitting on her immediately.

Lissa wasn't at all interested, or so we thought, at his obvious advances. In fact, she denied him and any attempts of even talking to her every time.

Now here she is asking if he's dating Halle, not realizing she's never met Halle or who she is to me.

"If they were, would it bother you?"

"No," she replies sharply, rolling her eyes as she kneels on the floor to wipe up the mess.

She's as bothered by their flirting as I am. I want to laugh at how stubborn she can be.

She doesn't look at me as she continues to busy herself with remaking the spilled drink and lining them all onto her tray.

"Lissa," I say, interrupting her. She huffs out a breath, blowing a strand of hair in front of her face as she looks up at me. The same moment she does that, we hear another round of laughs behind us, drawing our attention back to Halle and Brannon.

Flexing my jaw, I shake my head wanting to yell at Brannon to lay off when I think about his words from earlier tonight about how it's my fault she's on the market anyway. It's true and I can't exactly go around telling Halle who she can't be with.

Turning my attention back to Lissa, she plasters a fake smile on her face as she moves the tray into her hands.

"What's up?"

"For the record, they aren't together," I say, pausing to make sure she hears me. "Remember Halle, the girl from back home I told you about?"

When Lissa and Adam broke up, she was upset. She tried to hide it, she can play it off well, but when I found her broken down in the cooler one night after a text message he had sent her, I opened up to her about the one that got away.

It takes her a minute, but her eyes widen as she remembers who that is as she looks back over at them and then back to me.

"That's her?"

"Yep," I say. "If I had to guess, they are both trying to get under our skin. Trust me, I know because even though they keep talking, he hasn't been able to keep his eyes off you."

"Of course, he can't," she mocks, tossing her hair over her shoulder. "God, he is such a pain in the ass," she curses, adjusting the tray on her arm as she saunters over to the table.

I want to laugh as Brannon eyes her the entire way over. She knows it, too, as she adds an extra swing to her hips.

Stubborn woman.

chapter eleven

HALLE

"**I**s Graham going to come to his senses someday and realize what a great catch he let go of?" Brannon says, leaning in close as he whispers low enough so only I can hear him.

I'm not stupid and neither is he. I don't know who the girl is that Graham has been chatting it up with, but whoever it is, she's someone Brannon doesn't want him talking to either.

"Probably not," I joke, just as she walks away from Graham toward our table with a tray full of our drinks.

"Well, if it isn't the firecracker herself."

For a second, I think she didn't hear him, as she begins serving the drinks to everyone around the table. I take a sip of my martini, feeling the warmth from the alcohol rush through me.

Once she finishes unloading the drinks, she slides the tray under her arm as she focuses her attention back on Brannon. I know that look, she's letting him know now she's not at all amused by him and I want to laugh.

"Did you decide what you wanted to order?"

Brannon leans forward with his elbows on the table. Graham pulls out a chair next to me, taking a seat at the end, flashing me a wink as he leans back getting comfortable.

"Hmm," Brannon says, knowing how much his prolonged response is driving her crazy.

"I'll let you continue to think on it," she says, as Brannon holds his hand up to stop her.

Her eyes narrow at him as she lets out a heavy sigh.

"I'll let you surprise me." He smiles.

I don't know whether to laugh or hold my breath at the grin that takes over her face.

"Sure thing," she says, dropping her smile as she turns and walks away.

"Well, that was interesting," I say, looking over at Brannon and back to Graham. "I don't think your friend likes Brannon much."

Brannon laughs. "She can play it off all she wants, but I think I'm breaking her down a little. Sooner or later, she'll fall in love with me."

"Good luck," Graham responds.

I want to be annoyed, I should be annoyed. Once again, I'm reminded of what he was doing when he left me, or maybe who he was doing.

I feel jealous and, honestly, I hate it. I don't get jealous, but when it comes to Graham Shaw, nothing is off limits.

I take a large gulp of my martini, not wanting to feel the way I'm feeling right now. As much as I hate turning to alcohol, I just want to numb everything and if I'm going to have to sit through the reminders of him walking away from me, I'd rather not feel a damn thing.

I take one last drink before setting the glass down. A shiver races over my body, the effects of the alcohol surging through me.

"You trying to get drunk?"

Graham looks at me, concern in his eyes. I know he hates when I drink but tonight, I don't really care.

"Not necessarily," I lie.

"Well, take it easy."

I want to tell him not to worry about me, but I see Lissa approaching with Brannon's drink, and all I care about is putting in another order.

"Your drink, sir." She smiles, setting the drink on the table.

Brannon looks down, then back up at her. "What is it?"

Lissa perches her hand on her hip before smiling smugly back at him. "That is an Adios Motherfucker!"

I cover my mouth to contain my laughter. This girl is my spirit animal.

"You're kidding me," Brannon deadpans.

"I don't think she is." I laugh.

"Enjoy," she replies sweetly, before she walks away.

Brannon growls, muttering something under his breath about her being a hellfire and having his hands full with her. He slides out of his seat and follows along behind her. I didn't even get to order my drink.

"If he's not going to drink this, I will."

Graham grabs my wrist in his hand, stopping me. "I think you're good for now. Don't you?"

Staring down at his grip on me, I want to fire back, but then he stands and pulls me up with him.

"It's been awhile," Graham intimates, leaning in close to me. "Why don't you show me your moves?"

If I wasn't feeling the effects of the alcohol already, I was feeling them now. Or it was the Graham effect. Good lord, he has a way of making me so wanton.

He pulls me along behind him. I hear Callum catcall behind us, followed by Mason yelling "finally." As soon as we approach the dance floor, he slows down, putting his arm around me as the crowd of people envelops us. People on the dance floor move. The beat of the music pulsating, almost like the way my body feels having Graham near.

When we're far enough away from the table, Graham stops and pulls me into his arms. Everything around us falls away, and it's just the two of us.

Wrapping his arms around me, his hands roam over my backside. Feeling his hands on me again with the limited space between us, it's heady. I don't want him to stop. Gripping the front of his shirt in my hands, I lean forward till there's only an inch separating our mouths.

It's a bold move. I know it and so does he. I'm tempting him because damn it, I want him so bad.

He leans in further. We're so close to kissing now, I can nearly taste him on my lips. The look of desire and sweat coat his face.

Digging my nails into his chest, I drag them down his front until I reach the waistband of his jeans. He bites his lower lip telling me he likes where this is going, but he doesn't move or stop me.

Turning, I press my back against him, grinding my ass against him. I can feel every inch of him, and the thought of having him again makes my legs weak with how much I want him.

"Halle," he breathes into my ear, pressing his hand against my stomach holding me against him.

We dance together off and on throughout the night and every time we do, it's like we somehow get closer. It makes me miss the times when I could kiss him and touch him. I almost feel like looking back on them now, I took those moments for granted.

Now I crave the chance to be near him in a way that is unhealthy for me. Like I'd go to lengths to have him around me that are not becoming, but I honestly don't give a damn.

Later that night, we both step off the elevator together. The sexual tension between us is so thick. I almost want to slow down and take my time getting to our doors, knowing this is the point when we will part ways, and I don't want our time together to end.

Standing in front of my door, Graham leans in and whispers "goodnight" against my ear. His lips drag along the edge of my ear. He pulls himself away, as he swipes the keycard to his room and disappears inside. My body feels the loss of him as soon as he's gone. I sigh against the door, immediately missing him and regretting the missed opportunity to kiss him.

I miss the feel of his soft lips on mine, the way his large hand would wrap over the side of my face, tangling his fingers in my hair.

It's evident he wanted to kiss me, and God, I wanted to kiss him too. Everything in me wanted to take what we've both been denying ourselves since I first saw him standing in my doorway weeks ago.

Flashing the keycard in the door, I rush inside and toss my purse on the bed. Looking in the mirror, I fix my hair and adjust the front of my dress, giving the girls a little bit of lift.

Walking back to the door that separates our rooms from each other, I quietly knock on it before stepping back and waiting. The nerves hit me, jitters breaking out over my body.

The lock on the door clicks just before Graham's face appears. His shirt is off and just like that the game's over. My resolve is gone, chucked somewhere behind me along with my plans to continue pushing his buttons making him regret leaving me.

"Something wrong?" he asks, his brow furrowing.

In this moment, all that is left standing there is just him and me. Pushing the door open all the way, I'm caught off guard when I find him with his pants unbuttoned and his boxer briefs peeking out from below his jeans.

"Yes, something's wrong. It's wrong how bad I want you, how bad I fucking need you right now," I say, running the palm of my hand over his chest.

His skin breaks out in goose bumps, as my finger traces his abs down to the edge of his boxer briefs. Wrapping my hand into the front of his jeans, I pull him closer to me.

He doesn't expect it, and I love how bold I feel. How it takes him by surprise, but I note the glimmer in his eyed telling me how much he loves it.

"What's more wrong is what I'm willing to do to make you put me out of my misery."

He lets go of the door, causing it to slam shut behind me, and just like that his hands are on me.

Wrapping his hands in my hair, he pulls my head back giving him access to my neck. He runs his nose along the column of my neck, whispering how good I smell and how much he wants to taste me.

He licks and nips his way up my neck and over to my ear.

"You need me to touch you, Halle?" he asks.

I'm so close to begging him that I'm half tempted to climb up his body and wrap my legs around him, just to feel some friction relief.

Pressing my back against the door, I run my hands over his chest again down to where his dick is straining against the front of his pants.

Wrapping my palm around him, he lets out a string of expletives before he grabs my arm and holds it above my head.

"Don't move," he says, holding my stare. "Cause I need you just as much as you need me."

I know Graham would never do anything to hurt me. That thought would never even enter my mind.

"This is about you," he sighs, running his hands down my arms over my chest. He squeezes my breast over the material of my dress. I can feel my nipples straining against the lace of my bra, begging for him to touch them.

"Where is the zipper?" he asks, as I turn my body to an angle showing him where the zipper is underneath my arm. He slides it down, careful not to ruin the material but urgent enough to not waste any time.

As soon as he sees the lace material of my bra, he whispers "fuck" to himself again before glancing up to look me in the eyes. He knows I wore this for a reason. Even if I told myself I wasn't going to give into him, there was always the chance that I would.

I knew how much he loved seeing me in lace and I loved seeing the look on his face when he did.

Letting the dress fall to the floor, I watch as Graham's six-four frame kneels in front of me. Kissing a path over my stomach, down to the apex of my thigh and back up to the lace material of my panties.

His nose grazes a path over the top of my mound and the slightest bit of contact is enough to make my legs feel like jelly beneath me.

The level of care he showed a moment ago is gone now, as he reaches out and rips the material away from my body. My jaw drops, as my panties fall to the floor along with my dress, before my eyes find Graham's once again. I can't be mad when I see the look of hunger and desire written on his face.

He is waiting for me to say something, to reprimand him for ruining my underwear. When he realizes it isn't going to come, he smiles as he moans and whispers, "Good girl."

Running his callused hand up my legs and over my thigh, he picks up my left leg and begins tracing kisses from my knee up the inside of my leg. Just before he reaches my pussy, he begins the descent back down my thigh again.

He does that several times before I feel like I am about to come out of my skin, but not once do I move my arms back down. Nope. I want to continue to obey his commands, to be his good girl, not wanting to find out what will happen if I don't.

I want him to put me out of my misery. To put out this fire he's started in me, that only he will ever be able to put out.

When he gets close to my pussy again, my pelvis begins seeking him out. Wrapping his hands around to my ass, he holds me close to him as he feathers a breath over my heated skin.

His cool breath on my wet skin leaves me whimpering, as I squeeze my eyes closed and tilt my head back against the door.

With one swipe of his tongue, I can see stars dance in front of me, as I start chanting his name praising him for how good he makes me feel. One of his fingers enter me, just barely, as his tongue continues to flick over my clit. Slowly, expertly.

One minute his finger will be there and the next it's gone. He knows what he is doing. Giving me just enough of what I want before taking it away. It is maddening but feels incredible all at the same time.

My orgasm starts to build from the moment his tongue touches me, but it is his finger slowly entering me and disappearing that keeps me on the brink. It's as if I've been left hanging on the edge of the cliff, waiting to fall.

I keep chanting his name and begging him "please" when his finger slowly enters me again, curling just enough. Just like that, I feel my body catapult over the edge leaving stars flashing before me as the aftershocks of my release jolt through me.

It is a good thing he has a hold of me, or I would've fallen over, left in a puddle on the floor of his hotel room.

Moving to stand, I can see his cock aching to break free from the confines of his jeans. I reach out for him, but he stops me. Grabbing my hand, kissing it as he lifts me up in his arms. My body relaxes into him, wrapping around his neck.

I mumble a soft "thank you" as he lowers me onto the bed, feeling the soft cotton of the bed sheets.

He bends down and presses a kiss against the edge of my mouth before whispering, "no, thank you," as my lids fall heavy, closing over my eyes.

chapter twelve

GRAHAM
eighteen years old

The feel of her warm breath glides along the side of my neck. The sun has long since gone down, leaving us standing beneath the starry night sky. Just her. Just her and me, alone together.

Sliding my hands along her sides, I pull her hips in closer, so she's pressed against me. The subtle moan that escapes her lips makes me crave the feel of them on mine.

Wrapping my fingers in her hair, I stare into her eyes for a moment before I give in and press my mouth roughly against hers.

She sighs softly, as her fingers slide along my cheek and into my hair, holding my head against her as she roughly pulls the strands.

Some days I feel like I can't get enough of her. When I wake up in the morning, she's the first thing I think about. When

I go to bed at night, she's the last thing on my mind. When we're together, I find myself being reckless out of the need to give her everything she wants. Just like I am now, standing outside in the middle of a dark field, ready and willing to give into her just to hear more of those sighs of contentment.

Her smile, her laugh, and her snarky sense of humor. She's everything. She pulls me out of the dark corners of my mind, and I fucking love her for it.

Her tongue brushes against my lower lip, eagerly seeking entrance into my mouth and I give into her. I give into her every damn time because this woman fucking owns me. She's everything that is good and right in this world.

I'd give her the world if she wanted. All she'd have to do is ask.

"Graham," she sighs again, and I can't help it. Brushing my thumb over the apple of her cheek, I pull back and look into her eyes before I press another kiss against her lips.

"Yes, sweetheart."

"Take me back to your house," she whispers, as she rubs her legs together.

I recognize the look of desire in her eyes, just as she roughly presses a kiss against my lips. Her quiet whimpers as her fingers claw against my neck, holding me in place.

We've both been drinking tonight. My mom had to pull a double shift at the bar tonight and likely won't be home until after two in the morning.

Sliding my hand into my pocket, I pull out my phone and break the connection with Halle to check the time on the screen. The time reads 12:14 a.m. and I curse the thought of having to call my cousin, Gage.

"I'll call Gage, have him come get us."

Halle drops her hands to her sides, just before she reaches up and runs the palms of her hands over her face. She doesn't like the idea of calling Gage for a ride anymore than I do, mostly because we both know the lecture that's going to ensue on the way home.

Talk about a buzz kill.

"'Ello," he grumbles into the phone. I'm not sure if he's just distracted or if he was asleep, so I cut to the chase quick.

"Gage, Halle and I are at a bonfire over at Mason's house for his graduation party and we, uh..." I pause, looking at Halle.

Halle's eyebrows are raised, like she's waiting for his rant to come on the other end of the phone. I flash her a wink, hoping to reassure her.

"We need a ride home, if you can."

"Graham..." he sighs. I hate hearing the disappointment, especially coming from him.

"You can save the lecture. I know, alright. At least I'm doing the responsible thing and asking you for a ride."

"Yeah, it takes balls to call a cop and ask for a ride when you've been drinking... underage," he says, drawing out the last part.

"So, does that mean you'll be here in twenty?"

"I'll call you when I'm almost there," he groans. I can hear his chair squeaking in the background, and I feel bad realizing he must still be at work. "I don't want to sit there waiting around for you or I'll break up the party myself."

I don't doubt for a second he would, so I reassure him we'll be ready. As soon as the line disconnects, I slip the phone back into my pocket and wrap my hands around Halle's waist pulling her to me.

"See, that was easy."

She laughs, tilting her head back to glance up at me. Holding her chin in my hand, I pull her lips back to mine and get lost in her.

"I can't wait to get back to your place," she whispers, her warm breath feathering over my wet lips.

"Mm," I hum, sliding my hand down the curve of her back, grabbing her ass and pressing her against me. "I can't wait to hold you tonight."

There's a peace that washes over me having her in my arms at night.

I don't even realize how long we stand here pressed against each other until my phone vibrates in my pocket. I know it's Gage, so I don't even bother looking at the screen as I swipe it to answer.

"We're waiting for you," I say, slipping my hand into Halle's and motion toward the front of the drive. The crowd of people in the distance is far enough away from the road that you wouldn't know what we're up to unless you drive all the way onto the Reid property.

Not wanting to leave Gage waiting, I opt to just send Mason a text message telling him I'll catch up with him tomorrow as Halle and I head toward the front of the house where the cars are parked.

"I'm just turning down Tucker Road," he says. "What the fuck?" he shouts. The sound of tires screeching in the background causes my adrenaline to spike.

"What the hell, man? Back the fuck up off me!" he yells.

"Graham, I'm on the way but this guy—" he cuts off again. I feel like I can hear my heart beating in my ears, as I clutch my phone into my hand.

My hand squeezes around Halle's, as she wraps hers around my arm as I hear her muffled words asking me if everything is alright.

"Gage, you alright?" I ask.

I hear him shout my name, followed by the sound of metal crunching on the other end of the phone before the call disconnects.

"Gage!" I shout, my voice growing hoarse as I hold my phone out in front of me. I quickly click on his name again, redialing is number as the line continues to ring and ring repeatedly in my ear.

"What happened?" Halle asks. There's a fear in her voice. It's the same fear I feel wrapping around my heart and squeezing it.

"I don't," my voice cracks, "I don't know."

Looking down the road, I look for a sign of his headlights in the distance, anything that would give me a clue that he's okay and what I just heard on the other end of the line was not what it seemed to be.

When I don't see him, the realization hits me like a ton of bricks as ice rushes through my veins.

"I have to go," I mutter out, dropping Halle's hand, as I take off running down the gravel driveway, cutting across the yard onto Tucker Road.

My chest heaves as my lungs struggle to pump air through my chest, as my feet pound against the pavement. The red and blue lights flashing in the distance, grow closer as my eyes turn blurry from the tears filling my eyes.

I don't think about anything. It's as if my mind is completely blank, which is good. I'm scared if I were to think about anything in this moment, I'd be pulled into the darkness. It's inevitable though.

My throat burns, as the sweat drips down my face, mixing with the tears. I make it there, just as the paramedics pull up at the scene.

I immediately recognize Kane, Brannon's brother, as he steps out of the driver's side of the ambulance. He must've seen me approaching because as soon as he's out, he quickly slams the door shut and stops me from coming any closer.

"Hey, buddy. We need you to stay back, okay? I know you're worried, I get it, but there's nothing you can do to help right now. Let us focus on helping him."

Forcing air into my chest, I attempt to swallow. I can hardly breathe, much less speak, as I nod my head and hold my hands up as I take a step back.

My eyes are wild, trying to look around them, for any sign of Gage and that he may be okay. I keep hoping I'll hear his voice, that I'll see him sitting there talking to the firefighters.

As I see them kneeling next to his vehicle, I realize in that moment it's not going to happen. The sound of metal crunching again, as they try to open the driver's side door is a sound I remember all too well, and just like that, my knees give out beneath me.

There's no stopping the storm that follows, as the tears pour down my face. The gravel cutting into my bare knees is a welcomed pain, a distraction from the impending fear in front of me.

If there is a God, I pray to him and ask for mercy on Gage. I don't ask for much, so it may seem greedy in this moment, but I promise it will be the last thing I ever ask if he'll just not take him away from me.

Watching as the firefighter throws his helmet on the ground in frustration, I know my fears have just been confirmed.

Kane turns around, approaching me. "Graham, man, I'm so sorry."

I hold my hand up to him, not wanting to hear him say what I already know.

The guilt that filters in is the same guilt that will torment me for years to follow. Staying in Arbor Creek is just a painful reminder of everything I've lost along the way. First my father, now Gage.

I'll be damned if I let the same thing happen to the two women I love more than life itself. They're better off without me.

chapter thirteen

HALLE

I hardly spoke to Graham the rest of our trip to Chicago. Or rather, I did my best to avoid him, which wasn't easy to do.

When I woke up the next morning, it was like the events from the last night played over and over on repeat in my head. Ever since he waltzed back into town looking like sex on a stick, I've fought against the urge to let it go one step further. I know Graham, I see the way he's holding himself back when he's around me. That night was a perfect example.

I just threw myself at him. I practically begged him like a cat in heat. He wouldn't even let me touch him, which is kind of mortifying when I think about it. I handled my embarrassment in the best way I knew how; I sunk my head under the comforter and sulked.

When I finally pulled myself out of bed, I promised myself not to think about it again. I reminded myself of the past; the way it hurt when he threw us away, the pain I felt when he ignored my attempts to talk to him after he left town, the way he acts as if all the time we spent together never happened. I let it be the reminder I need that going down this road again will only lead to heartache. Instead, I am going to put my focus on where it needs to be, which is on my family, friendships, and my career. One of my best friends is about to have her big day. No one deserves love more than Ellie and seeing the way Callum loves her and cares for her is another reminder of why I need to focus on the present.

The week leading up to the wedding has been a whirlwind. I didn't realize all the last-minute details that go into preparing. Now I know why Kinsley has been marching around with a damn clipboard, because if anyone else was left to planning, it would've been mass chaos.

After a short day at the salon, Kinsley and I drove together to Callum and Ellie's house for the rehearsal before meeting up with everyone for dinner. We had a girls' night planned with Ellie and Brea. You know, traditions and all where the bride is not supposed to see her groom.

"Alright, Callum, you can let us have her for one night. After tonight, you'll have her all to yourself," Kinsley says, as she steps around to the back of Ellie's car.

Callum presses his hands against the roof of the car, trapping Ellie in. Leaning forward, he presses a kiss against her lips as she wraps her arms around him, pulling him closer.

"Good lord, she's going to get pregnant right here in front of all of us," I jest, although it's highly possible. They haven't been able to keep their hands off each other all night. If we don't run off with her now, we're going to have a tough time separating them.

Callum growls, as he playfully kisses her cheek and down her neck, banding his arms around her, not wanting to let her go. Ellie laughs gleefully as I roll my eyes, looking over at Kinsley as I playfully stick my finger in my mouth like I'm gagging.

"Uhh, I need some wine for all this..." I motion my hands at them. "Love and stuff. I'm going to stop by Hudson's and grab some wine and I'll meet you guys and the lovebird back at our place."

Kinsley nods as Brea laughs, waving back. It's going to be a few minutes before they're able to pull Ellie away from Callum and into the car. It's best for all of us that I get a head start.

Kinsley's grandpa owns a grocery store in Arbor Creek, which happens to be where Ellie worked when she moved here last year. It's famously named after him, Hudson's. Since we have to drive further out of town to go to a bigger store, it makes it the perfect place to stop for nights like tonight.

I pull into the parking lot and slip into one of the spots out front. Clicking the lock on my door, I'm only able to get two steps in front of me before a car races into the parking lot cutting me off.

"What the hell?" I mutter, stopping myself before I let out a string of swear words.

It's not because I suddenly remember my manners, unlike the rude asshole who just about hit me. No, it's actually the exact opposite. I'd love to lay into the piece of shit standing in front of me, I just know better not to.

It's been a few weeks since I last saw Marc Krate outside of Brodie's. I honestly fully expected him to steer clear of me when he realized not only was Graham back in town, but he was there at Brodie's with me that night.

"That's not a nice way to greet someone, Halle," he says. His lip sticks out from the tobacco stuffed inside his lip. He spits, narrowly missing my foot in the process.

Squinting my eyes at him, I press my lips into a thin line in an attempt to keep me from firing off at the mouth.

Holding onto the strap of my purse, I adjust it on my shoulder as my eyes glance around me. I'm not some damsel in distress, but I get an overwhelming sense of uneasiness around this prick. The sooner I can wrap this up, the better.

"Can I help you with something?"

The words come out sharply. He's grating on my nerves and I really have no patience for dealing with him right now. Or ever.

"That's so kind of you to ask. Actually, you can," he states, leaning forward as he looks around the parking lot.

The knot in my stomach tightens. Squeezing my hand tighter around the leather strap, I contemplate climbing back in my car. He's blocking me in now though. There's no way out of here without jumping the parking block in front of my car, which would likely do some damage.

"Spit it out," I reply curtly.

The smile on his face turns sinister, and I immediately wish I would've just shut up.

"You see that boyfriend of yours lately?"

It dawns on me the irony in his question. Surely if he thought Graham was still my boyfriend, he'd know the answer. After the threat he gave him last time he came around, I wonder why he'd be asking me this of all questions.

"Obviously."

He chuckles to himself as his eyes rake over my body. His obvious perusal of my body makes me feel disgusting, dirty.

"Good." He smiles again. "You can give him a message for me then. You tell him if I catch his boys following me again, I'll see to putting him six feet under next to that cousin of his. You hear me?"

My throat goes dry as the words hit my ears. He smiles again, spitting on the ground as bile rises up my throat.

I don't doubt for a second after we saw him at Brodie's, Graham did some digging into Krate. We all see his name in the paper. It's no secret the trouble he's been getting himself into.

"Alright." My voice cracks. "I'll tell him."

I'm about to ask him to leave when a large black diesel truck pulls up behind him, parking next to me. I don't recognize the vehicle at first, but I relax a bit when I spot Maverick walk around the back stopping next to me.

"Everything alright here?"

He must feel how uncomfortable I am. I'm practically pleading with him to help me, to get me out of here and away from him.

"We're good. Nothing for you to be poking your nose into," Krate says, but I pick up his double meaning. Something tells me he's aware Maverick's one of the guys who's following him, but if he does, he doesn't say anything.

"You two have a good night," Krate says, a sarcastic smile lines his mouth as he turns to climb back in his car. "You remember what I said, Halle."

He winks at me, just before rolling the window back up. The tint is so dark once it's all the way up, I'm left staring at my scared reflection alongside Maverick's stone-cold face next to me.

We both watch as he slowly drives to the back of the parking lot, disappearing down the alley.

"You okay? What'd he say to you?" Maverick questions, looking me over. There's an edge of concern laced in his tone.

He moves to take a step closer to me, catching me off guard, so I take a step back pressing me against my car door.

"Whoa, Halle. It's okay. It's just me."

"He just said..." I stutter, running my hand over my forehead. I feel light-headed and dizzy. Like all the adrenaline is now hitting me and I need to sit down. "He said he knows Graham has been poking around in his business, having people follow him or something. He said he wants him to back off or he'll..."

I can't even finish my sentence. The words are caught in my throat, unable to come out.

"Or he'll what, Halle? What'd he say?"

Maverick reaches out, rubbing his hand over my shoulder in an attempt to reassure me. "He's not going to hurt you, okay? That much I can promise you. I just need you to tell me what he said."

"He said if he doesn't back off, he'll put him six feet under next to Gage."

Tears trail down my face, and I don't even bother to wipe them away. I know he understands the weight of those words. Anger transforms the look on his face, as he clenches his jaw.

"Motherfucker," he growls, gritting his teeth.

"Whatever you guys are up to, please stop. It's not worth it. It's not worth making him mad or risking your lives. I've lost Graham once, I don't want to think about losing him forever."

I get choked up saying that last word. Shouldering past Maverick, I cover my mouth trying to get my emotions in check. I just want to get in and out of the store, then go home. I focus on the sound of my sandals against the cement ignoring him calling out my name to try and stop me.

Right now, I just want to drown my problems in a glass of wine and forget everything.

chapter fourteen

GRAHAM

All I could think about after I got off the phone with Maverick was Halle. Was she okay? I just wanted to pull her into my arms and hold her.

I tried calling her, only for the call to go straight to voice mail. She texted me back saying she was having a girls' night and couldn't talk but assured me she was alright. She had to know after the last time, it bothered me.

Considering she hardly looked at me the entire way back from Chicago, much less spoke to me, I had a feeling she regretted the night in my hotel room.

Today is Callum and Ellie's wedding. It's beautiful outside, making a perfect day for them. I spend most of the morning and early afternoon with Brannon, finishing the setup down at the pavilion overlooking the pond behind Callum and Ellie's house. I understand now why they decided to get married here. It's peaceful and intimate.

When we're finished there, we make the trip over to Callum's parents' place. When Callum decided to build his house, he ended up buying land from his mom and stepdad, Randy. They own several acres out here with a barn separating the two properties.

Wanting to keep with the same private and intimate reception, they cleared out the barn and opted to use it as a makeshift dance floor. Brannon and I help set up tables around the outside with a table along the front for the bride and groom, and their wedding party. It's almost surreal seeing the transformation.

Once everything is set up and ready to go, I race home to shower quickly and change into my dress shirt and slacks before heading back to Callum's house. The girls are still inside getting ready. The guys take over the oversized garage where Callum spends a lot of his time fixing up his dirt bike and truck.

Cars are parked along the long gravel drive, leading up to their house. I watch as people mill around. Kinsley's brother, Kolton, is stepping in as an usher helping seat people.

Knocking lightly on the door, I hear the cheers from the guys as I peek my head inside as they all shout "Graham!"

If I had to guess, they've been biding their time until it's GO TIME by throwing back a few beers. Mason and Wes are standing off to the side, laughing about something as Callum and Brannon are near the front of the garage. Callum has an odd sense of peace on his face, and I'm not even surprised when I see him clutching a bottle of water.

The nerves are evident on his face, but I admire that he's not slinging back beers to cover them up.

"How you feelin', man? You ready?" I walk up to Callum, clapping him on the back.

"Hell, yes," he says, running his hands through his hair as he pulls his phone out of his pocket to check the time. "I've been ready. As much as I love you guys and all, I'm ready to get the fuck out of this garage and make that woman mine."

I laugh at his honesty.

"People are starting to get here. It will be go-time before you know it."

We hear a knock on the door again, just as Hudson peers his head inside.

"Hudson," Callum greets him. Hudson may be Kinsley's grandfather, but it's no secret that since Ellie moved to Arbor Creek that he's developed quite a bond to her.

While I'm still getting to know Ellie after moving back home, Mason's told me a lot about her and their relationship. It's no secret that before she met Callum and moved here, she had a rough go at life. She's the definition of strength, after all she's been through.

"How's she doing?" Callum asks, folding Hudson into a hug.

The time I've spent away has changed him some. The salt and pepper hair he once had is now covered with a steel gray. He's still every bit the man I knew and remember growing up. Hudson was the kind of grandparent to Kinsley and Kolton that seemed like they were your grandparents, too. He may have slowed down some over the years, but he's still every bit of the man he was then.

"Oh, she's doing good. I think she's like you, ready to get this going. Ready to see you." He smiles, reassuring Callum. "She looks beautiful, Callum."

The tears form in Hudson's eyes and I feel like I'm interrupting a private moment that's meant to stay between them two.

Glancing over at Callum, he releases a slow breath as he runs his knuckle under his eye as he blinks away the tears.

"I bet she does. I'm sure she's already told you this, a few times if I had to guess," Callum laughs, "but I just want to say thank you for being here today. I can't tell you how much it means to her."

Hudson rests his hand on Callum's shoulder, squeezing it as he looks around at each of us. Mason and Wes have stopped their conversation, joining us.

"Ellie is like a daughter to me. I wish more than anything it was her father who was here, walking her down the aisle. Since he can't be, it is my honor to stand in for him and give her away."

Callum reaches forward and wraps Hudson in a hug. They exchange words and each of us give them their moment.

When they step back, Hudson looks back around the room at all of us and laughs. "Golly, you boys clean up well. It won't be too long before each of you are standing in Callum's shoes."

He chuckles, looking around at us before he reaches out to shake Callum's hand.

"I'm going to get back to our girls. We have just a few minutes until it's time for all of you to get out there."

"It's good to have you home, son," Hudson says, clapping his hand on my shoulder. He winks at me before he walks out the door.

"I think that's my cue to head out there too."

Callum, while he's one of my good friends, has a closer relationship to Wes and Brannon. Growing up, they were his two best friends. It made sense for the two of them to stand next to him, along with his brother, Mason.

I follow the guys out, leaving them to head down to the pavilion as I take a seat, waiting for the wedding to start. When the music starts, I turn in my seat. I watch as my friends walk down the aisle one at a time, the last of the group is Halle with her hand wrapped around Brannon's forearm.

She looks beautiful, like a dream, as she walks slowly down the aisle. She fights back a smile at something Brannon says to her, before she squeezes his arm. Her eyes are bright with the happiness radiating off her.

The champagne color dress combined with her tan skin gives her the look like she's glowing, and I can't help but stare at her, even when her and Brannon separate and she takes her spot behind Kinsley.

There's hardly a dry eye in the room, as everyone watches Ellie walk down the aisle with Hudson by her side. This time Callum doesn't even attempt to hide his emotions, as the tears stream down his face.

As soon as she reaches him, he presses a kiss passionately against her lips. Hudson clears his throat, reminding him he's not supposed to do that just yet, which earns him a few laughs and makes Ellie smile.

You can feel the love between the two of them. The entire time, I'm unable to keep my eyes off Halle. It's hard not to picture us up there, her standing before me looking like the angel she is, and I'm like Callum, unable to resist the urge to pull her into my arms and thank God for giving me her forever.

Then, I remind myself that the future we had laid out before us was changed, and the only person to blame for it now is myself.

We listen as the pastor talks about loving each other in the face of hard times. I look over at Halle and watch her as she glances down at her flowers, running her hand underneath her eye again, before she peeks over at me.

She looks surprised when she finds me staring back at her, but this time she doesn't look away.

"I'm sorry," I mouth to her.

She gives me a sad smile, turning to look back at Callum and Ellie.

We both watch as the pastor asks them to recite their vows. When he announces them as husband and wife, our eyes once again find each other's. This time I hope the look on my face says everything I can't say in that moment.

Halle deserves better than anything I could ever give her. She deserves someone who would give her the world. While I can't give her all those things, I can promise her one thing. I will love her more than anyone ever possibly could.

All these years, Halle never once gave up on me. When I walked away from her, she never turned her back on me. She never stopped loving me. She doesn't have to say the words, I know it with everything in me.

While I can't go back and fix what I took away from her, from us, these past five years, I can promise her today and everyday forward that I'll be the man she deserves.

Until I found her, I never knew what loving someone meant. Now I need to prove to her that I'll never let her go again.

chapter fifteen

HALLE

"Your vows today, Callum, they were so beautiful. And Ellie looks stunning and happy. This entire day, I'm just so happy for you both."

Our hips sway to the music, as we both glance over at her. Her hand is wrapped around Wes's forearm, their other hand wrapped together, as they dance slowly to the music.

Wes spins her before pulling her back into his arms. I'm not sure if it's the move or something he said that leaves her blushing, as she glances over at Callum.

"Thank you." He smiles, as he stares back at her. You can feel how much it means to him seeing her happiness, her laughter.

Everything about their love just fills me with so much hope that someday I'll find what they have found together.

"She means the world to me. I can't imagine my life without her now, you know. I'm the luckiest bastard in the world." Callum's soft laugh reaches his eyes as he steals a glance at his new bride.

Ellie rests her cheek against Wes's shoulder as she smiles back at Callum. He winks at her, just before he whistles at his friend to get his attention.

"I don't mind you dancing with my girl and all, but can you maybe put a little distance between the two of you?"

Callum grins and plays off that he's joking, but we all know there's a little bit of truth to his comments. Ellie rolls her eyes playfully as she blows him a kiss, just as Brannon approaches, asking to cut in.

"Does she have any idea where you're planning to take her yet? I'm surprised you've managed to keep it a secret for this long."

Callum chuckles. "If she has any idea, she hasn't let on. She likes to try to guess, but so far, it's remained a secret. It's the first time I've ever kept anything from her. When I see her face, it will all be worth it."

When Callum proposed to Ellie, she told him yes but made him promise to keep the wedding small. She's not at all into things being big and flashy. That's what I love about her. She holds so much value in the people close to her. Callum, on the other hand, wanted to share with the world Ellie was going to be his wife. When she explained to him it wasn't important to her and would mean more for their family and close friends to be there, he couldn't deny giving her everything she wanted.

Ellie didn't have a lot of family. I think the thought of planning a wedding brought on the reminder of the people who would be absent on her big day.

I think Callum's one of few men in history to completely plan the wedding. Ellie helped with some of it. like dress shopping and certain décor pieces. The rest was all him. Ellie had been through enough leading up to their engagement. He knew the trial proceedings putting away the man who hurt her, affected Ellie deeply. He didn't want to add any stress to what he wanted to be the happiest time of their life.

Looking around the old rustic barn, I'm just in awe of what they accomplished. It looks like something you'd see featured in a country living magazine.

The sound of a throat clearing behind us draws my attention back to the present, to Graham standing in front of us.

"Do you mind if I cut in?" Graham asks, looking from me to Callum.

"Who am I to stand in the way of you dancing with Callum on his big day," I joke, taking a step back, sweeping my hand in front of me.

I want to laugh at the look on his face, as his eyes narrow at me.

"Get over here." Graham gives a flirtatious growl, and I can't help the giggle that escapes.

"Alright, alright. Kinsley, looks like it's your turn." I smile, looking over my shoulder to where Kinsley stands talking to Brea, waiting in line for their turn at dollar dances.

Graham's arms wrap around me, nearly taking all the air right out of me. The feel of his broad chest and the smell of his woodsy scent makes me dizzy.

The song changes, playing to Jason Aldean's "You Make It Easy" as I press my cheek against his arm. I close my eyes, focusing on the steady beat of my heart trying to take my mind off Graham and the way my stomach flutters being in his arms again.

Graham tilts his head forward, pressing his face into the crook of my neck. His warm breath feathers over my collarbone, and for a moment, I swear I feel his lips brush against my skin. Goose bumps break out over my body, forcing me to squeeze my eyes closed tighter as I force myself to breathe.

I shiver as he traces his lips up the column of my neck near my ear. His warm breath makes my heart stop beating and I hold my breath, waiting for what he's about to do next.

"You look so beautiful, Halle."

His hands clench my waist tighter, holding me to him. He leans back, wrapping his hand along the side of my face, brushing my hair back in the process.

"Look at me," he whispers, as I slowly open my eyes to stare up at him.

His wall is down. All his emotions are laid out before me. I don't know what to do, what to say. So, I do what's best for the both of us, and for once, I just shut up. I wait for him to say whatever it is he's been wanting to say, while praying in the process he doesn't crush me.

"I'm sorry," he says, pausing for a moment to take a deep breath. He looks somewhere behind me, his eyes become distant. He's lost in thought before snapping out of it, falling back on mine.

"I'm sorry for not walking you out to your car at Brodie's like I wanted to, for not being with you at Hudson's when Krate approached you again. I'm sorry for…"

I can feel the weight of this bearing down on him. This isn't just about the present, but so much more.

Pressing my hand to his chest, I want to tell him it's okay, he doesn't have to bring it up, but the words are out of his mouth before I can.

"I'm sorry I left you, Halle. I'm sorry I feared losing you too. I thought I was doing right by you, letting you go. After we lost Gage, I felt like I failed him. I couldn't bear the thought of failing you. It would kill me if something ever happened to you, Halle. Do you understand me?"

His thumb traces along the curve of my cheek and I realize then he's catching my tears, wiping them away.

"I hate to see you cry. You're too beautiful to be crying."

Rubbing my hand over his forearm, I whisper a soft "hey" urging him to look at me.

"It's okay. I'm okay, I promise."

He nods his head but keeps his gaze down.

"I'd give you my heart, beating in my chest, if it meant protecting yours."

Wrapping my hands around his neck, I pull him closer to me. His heart is hammering in his chest, pulsing like a drum, as I press my lips against his neck.

"Graham, it's okay. I'm right here. I'm not going any-where."

It takes him a moment, but I can hear the breath he's holding ease out of him as his arms tighten around me. We stand like this for a while, in the middle of the dance floor, holding each other. Even with our close friends here with us, dancing around us, it's like nothing else exists.

When the song changes to something with a faster pace, Graham leans back away from me as he cups his hands on the sides of my face.

"Will you come somewhere with me?"

I simply nod my head, when on the inside I'm screaming, "Yes, you big idiot. I'd go anywhere with you."

He eases his hand down my arm, wrapping our fingers together as he leads me off the makeshift dance floor and out to the door at the back of the barn.

Callum's mom and stepfather own the property, but Callum and Ellie's house is visible as it sits in the distance. There's a small creek in the back separating the two. We used to come down here all the time when we were younger.

It's getting late now. The sun has long since gone down. The lanterns lining the outside of the barn give us enough light to lead our way. Other than that, it's just us and the moon shining bright overhead. Graham and I don't speak to each other as we walk, but I am taken by surprise when a few yards away there's a blanket laid out on the ground.

"Will you sit here with me and just let me hold you again?"

I swear, he's stolen my heart again.

"Of course," I say, as he unbuttons the front of his jacket, laying it on the ground. He adjusts his dress pants, as he sits down leaving his legs open for me to sit between.

I lower myself, pressing my back against his chest. His arms envelope me in a hug, holding me close to him. He rests his chin on my shoulder, pressing his lips in a line from my shoulder up to my neck.

"Maverick told me what happened, what Krate said to you outside of Hudson's the other night. I wish you would've called me."

"Graham—" I say, stopping him. I'm frustrated and don't want to talk about this again.

"No, listen. I'm sorry, I just need to say this and then we'll put it to rest."

Letting out a sigh, I ease back against him and let him get this off his chest. No matter what I say, he won't let it go until he does.

"I wish you would've called me and told me what happened. After that night at Brodie's, I thought I made it clear if he does it again, I want to know about it."

"You think I didn't think about calling you a hundred times? I tried, Graham, I tried."

"You tried?" he asks, confused. "I didn't have a missed call from you."

"I'm not talking about just last night, I'm talking about over the past five years. I tried calling you. I tried reaching out to you, checking in to see how you were doing. In the beginning, I did tell myself you were hurting after losing Gage, but the more I tried to talk to you, for you to only deny me, I just gave up. So, forgive me for not racing to you when something happens and for thinking you'd be there for me. I've tried that before, and it didn't get me anywhere."

"Fuck, I'm sorry."

"I know you are, Graham, I get it. I know you're sorry. It doesn't change that I've been without you for the past five years. It doesn't change the fact every time I've needed you, you haven't been there. Did you even know I lost my

Grandma Mary last spring? You think I didn't want to call you then? I've been trying to just get through life not having you around, okay? You're not the only one who's lost people, Graham. You're not the only one who's been through shit. It doesn't give you an excuse or an out to give up on the people who've been there for you since day one."

I unclasp his hands from around my waist and push myself to stand, taking a step away from him. I look around for my sandals, wanting to just get away from him and go back to the reception.

"No, stop," he pleads, reaching his hand out as he fumbles to stand. "Wait, please. Dammit, Halle."

"Wait for what, Graham? Huh? Wait for you? I've done that already. I've wasted five years waiting on you, hoping you'd come back for me. I've hoped all along I'd wake up, thinking one day this would all be a terrible fucking dream. But it's not, okay? It's real life, this is reality. This is who we are now. We can't sit out here, staring up at the sky thinking we can go back to the way things were before. It's not that fucking easy."

"Don't you think I know that? God, Halle, don't you think I haven't thought about how I wish we could go back? If I could go back and change everything, I would."

"It's not that easy, Graham! You're not listening to me!" I yell, holding my hands up to my head.

"Nothing in life is easy, Halle. Nothing."

Behind Graham, I see Kinsley run out the barn door. Her eyes are wide and frantic as she looks around presumably for us.

"What is wrong with you two? Why are you yelling?"

Rolling my eyes, I look back at Graham. I want to yell at him for making me so damn frustrated. I'm standing in a fucking field shouting at him about the past and everything we can't change.

Graham reaches up, running his hands through his hair as he turns to look back at Kinsley. "Sorry, Kins. Everything's fine. We're just talking."

Kinsley looks back at me. I can read the question in her eyes. She trusts Graham, but she wants to make sure I'm alright too.

"We're fine, Kins. Sorry, we just got carried away and forgot where we were."

"Well, everyone in here heard you so you may want to remember before you carry on. We're about to cut the cake though, so if you want some you may want to come back in soon."

"Yeah," I sigh, "I'll be back in there in a minute."

With a head nod, Kinsley disappears back into the barn, pulling the door shut behind her giving us a little privacy. Maybe she doesn't trust we can keep it down, who knows.

"Halle, I'm sorry. I didn't bring you out here to dredge up old feelings or argue with you. I just wanted to forget everything that's happened, everything going on right now and just be with you. Just you and me. You always had a way of making me forget all the bullshit going on around me. I just needed to feel that again. I needed you."

Whatever is going on in his life is starting to wear on him. For the first time tonight, I notice the bags under his eyes and the tiredness weighing on his face. He still looks every bit of handsome he's always been, but there's a lost look to his eyes. I feel bad for adding to it even though we needed to talk about this.

"Is it your mom? Is she okay?"

"Yeah, she's fine. I promise. She misses you though. She's been asking about you."

I feel bad, it's been a while since I've been by to see her. I knew Graham was home and, to be honest, I was staying away for that reason. I hate myself for it now.

"What is it then? Is it about Krate? Maverick said you guys hadn't been following him, that he's probably on drugs and paranoid. Is that true?"

"Halle, it's nothing you need to worry about. I promise, everything is fine. Just things have been stressing me out at work since the opening. I've had some long nights with my mom, but I can assure you she's okay. Can you please just sit with me for a little bit? Then, we'll go back inside, and I'll get you some cake."

He holds out his hand to me and like the fool that I am, I go back to him. Every damn time I go running back to him.

"I never did thank you for that night in Chicago," he whispers, pulling me close to him again. He must see the confusion on my face as I stare up at him.

"For which part exactly?"

"For coming to me, that night after we got back to the hotel from Velvet."

I want to wince at the mention of that night, the embarrassment of how it all went down. God, it was like I couldn't help myself anymore. I needed him so badly.

"You are so fucking sexy, Halle. Dear God," he moans, and I swear my heart drops at the sound. He pulls me close to him again, as his hand wraps around my waist, anchoring me to him. "It took everything in me not to take you right there. I wanted to," he groans, tilting his head up toward the sky. "Fuck, I wanted to take you so damn bad. It took every bit of willpower left in me to carry you back to your room and put you to bed. Watching you fall apart like that for me, giving me a piece of you after all this time."

Raking my nails down his chest, I stare up at him, waiting for him to look back down at me. The need I feel churning in me now, racing through me, is running wild.

I want him so damn bad.

"Graham," I moan. "I need you."

chapter sixteen

GRAHAM

My head whips down, meeting her gaze, and there it is. There it fucking is.

Need is written all over her face, as her legs move beneath the fabric of her dress. She's turned on, aching for me, and she's rubbing those sexy as fuck legs together looking for some relief to the burn she's feeling inside her.

"Fuck, yeah, you do, baby," I breathe out, feeling my cock grow just looking at the glossy look in her eyes. "C'mere."

I pull her down on the blanket so she's on her knees sitting in front of me. Lying back, I ball my jacket into a makeshift pillow, pulling her so she's positioned over the top of me.

She doesn't wait for direction as she climbs on top of me and I can't help the string of swear words that follow as she positions her heat over the top of my dick. Even with my pants acting as a barrier between us, I can feel how wet she is as I rake my hands up her thighs.

When my fingers meet the lace material of her panties, I don't even try to hold in the moan. The way she bites down on her lower lip, loving the way my body reacts to her.

If there's anyone capable of taking my breath away, it's Halle. Seeing her standing in front of me in lace? That's one way to bring me to my knees. God. Damn.

"You wear these for me?" I ask, knowing how much I fucking love seeing her in lace. So fucking beautiful and delicate. She looks fucking beautiful in anything she wears, but there is a softness about seeing her in lace that brings me to my knees.

She nods her head, and I can't help but groan, knowing I was right. She can sit here and act like she doesn't want me. She can deny it all she wants, but she knows as well as I do, there is no stopping the pull we feel toward one another.

Sliding my finger beneath the edge of her panties, she leans back further giving me better access to her aching center. When my thumb slips across her, pressing against her swollen clit, I feel like I'm seconds away from coming in my fucking pants.

"Ooh, shit," she moans, throwing her head back as she grinds her pussy down on my thumb.

I continue to rub circles as she rubs her pussy over me. The movement, back and forth over my dick, is enough to drive me to the edge. I squeeze my eyes shut, trying to focus on her and her pleasure.

Her tentative hand reaches between us grabbing onto the belt buckle of my pants causing my eyes to shoot open meeting hers.

"I need to feel you, Graham," she whispers. Her tongue skates out, dragging a slow line across her lip, as she lets out a heavy "please."

It's nearly my undoing.

We stop for a second, as her hands reach between us, hurrying to free me from my pants. She quickly stands, stepping out of her underwear, and kicks them off near me before reaching forward to pick up the front of her dress.

It's a move so forward, so like Halle. When we were together, she would never hide herself from me. Her confidence, she wore it like a skin. It's what I loved most about her. How comfortable she was with herself and around me.

Watching her bare herself to me, in the middle of the field with nothing but the soft glow from the lanterns in the distance, I can't help but love her even more. She doesn't shy away from anything, never with me.

Positioning herself back over me, I watch as she lowers herself and her bare pussy over me.

"God, yes," she quietly moans, as she slides her pussy over my dick in one quick motion.

Her pussy tightens around me and let out a heavy breath, trying to rein in some restraint before I end this far too quickly. It's been too long since we've been together, and I want to drag this out for as long as I possibly can.

Sitting up, she wraps her legs around my back as I kiss her chest, holding her to me.

Her fingers drag along the nape of my neck, into my hair as she pulls on the strands.

"This, right here," I moan. "I've missed watching you fall apart for me."

The rest of the words are left there, dead on my lips as her mouth crashes down on mine. Her body rocks against mine, taking what she needs from me. Our hips crash back and forth as we race to the edge, needing to feel more of each other but never getting enough.

"Graham," she moans, her mouth open as she eagerly rides me sucking in every bit of air around us.

My fingers drag along the front of her dress, feeling her bare breast beneath the loose fabric. Pulling the strap down, freeing her from the confines, I groan seeing her rosy nipple peak from the cool night air.

Wrapping my lips around her, I suck and lick, alternating back and forth as she begs me for more and praises me with every yes. Her fingers wrap around the back of my head, holding me to her as she continues to ride me.

It's the little noises she makes combined with the steady motion that brings me racing to the edge.

"Halle," I moan against her chest, sliding my hands beneath her dress, grabbing onto her bare ass, holding her against me.

"I'm close, baby, tell me you're close."

I don't want to finish without her with me.

"I'm almost..." she mutters, her words coming out broken and breathy.

Reaching my hand between us, I run my thumb over her clit as she says my name again.

"Come for me, baby," I whisper, leaning up to kiss her.

Holding her face in my hand as her body clenches around me, we both fall over the edge together. She tilts her head back, as the aftershocks of her release race through her.

Pressing my lips against her chest, I feel the steady beat of our hearts together. Only mine feels like it's beating again for the first time in five years.

chapter seventeen

HALLE

All week I feel like I've been lost in a daze, thinking about how good it was to be with Graham again. The times we spent together when we were young are permanently etched in my memory. When he left, it was like I held onto those moments because they were the only thing I had left.

At night, I'd lie awake in bed and think about him. Those memories flashed through my mind like a camera reel. I'd replay the nights after football games when we'd drive down to the cliff. We'd go there if we wanted to hang out somewhere away from our house, where our parents seemed to always be eyeing us. I'd think about the nights when he'd sneak into my house just to lie next to me, holding me when I slept.

Those memories were always the hardest. I ached to feel his arms around me again.

That's why when he led me down to the pond and asked me to sit with him, I couldn't say no. We both know that so much still needs to be said between us, so much hurt from the past, about why he left. It's not something we can get over in a day, but I do think it was the first step to healing the pain that is still there buried.

I know he's trying, and it means a lot to me to see his name lighting up my phone. Every morning I've woken up to a text message from him and every night I've gone to bed with his voice telling me goodnight in my ear. We spent two hours on the phone Tuesday night.

For so long I thought it would be hard to visit Chicago and hear about what he has spent his time doing over the last five years. I got to listen as he shared with me about what it was like working at Velvet, living with Mason, and how all of this led him to opening Compass Security.

Taking a seat in my salon chair, I scroll through my Instagram feed looking at pictures Callum has been posting of Ellie lying on the beach in Maui. She looks so beautiful and relaxed under an umbrella, the sun beating down on her as she holds her arm up to block out the sunlight as she beams at Callum.

Halle: The photos of Callum and Ellie are making me jealous. I'm ready to leave on a jet plane to somewhere far from here.

Graham: Take me with you. It'll be a long night for me at the office, but I love the thought of a tropical vacation with you.

Grinning, I use my foot to spin my salon chair in circles until I come to a stop facing Kinsley. She just wrapped up with a client.

"Ugh, I don't know how you can do that. Just watching you sometimes makes me nauseous."

Giggling, I use my toe to push off, spinning me in circles again.

"I'm easily amused sometimes," I say with a laugh.

"You're more like a big child."

"Yeah, well, you're as serious as Mrs. Maven."

She clearly doesn't appreciate the comparison to our ninth-grade biology teacher. Seriously, her class was like the opposite of fun. She sucked all the fun right out of you in one big *whoosh*.

She halts her movement, glancing over her shoulder narrowing her eyes at me.

"That's not funny," she replies, flicking her tongue.

The chair spins to a slow halt, as I use my toe again to push enough so that I'm facing Kinsley. Her back is to me and I watch as she scrolls through her phone, before she tosses it to the side with a huff.

"I was kidding, Kins. Geez. Everything alright?"

Tossing everything on her counter into her drawer, she slams it shut. Turning, she plops down in her salon chair facing me.

"Yeah, everything's fine. I just haven't heard from Wes all day, and it's starting to bug me how little we talk to each other anymore. I'm sure it's nothing but sometimes it bothers me."

"You know he loves you. I'm sure it's not intentional, he's just been busy." I smile, reassuringly. I know after talking to Brannon, they've been super busy at their shop.

She contemplates it for a minute and I want to ask her what she's so worried about. She pulls her phone out of her purse, checking it. Drumming her fingers on the counter of her station, she flashes her eyes up at mine.

"Yeah, you're right." She pauses, sounding unsure of her answer. She takes a deep breath, looking lost in thought. I want to shake her, ask her what she's so worried about.

"Kins, you sure that's it? Talk to me."

"Do you think he'd ever cheat on me?"

I nearly choke, practically falling out of my seat. "Are you serious?"

"Yeah... I mean, we have hardly spent time together lately. For a while, I used Callum and Ellie's wedding as a way of keeping my mind off it. He blew off seeing me earlier this week. God, I just sound like this insecure twit."

She runs her hands through her hair, shaking her head. "He's just been acting so weird. I was looking forward to seeing him that night too. I spent extra time just getting ready, I had ordered out dinner and everything. He called me and said he was on his way home, he was just too tired."

Turning her head toward me, she looks at me as tears fill the brim of her eyes. She blinks them away, letting out a slow breath again.

"Too tired? I mean, really?"

"Okay, forget going by and seeing him. Let's go home, get drunk on wine, and binge watch Friends. It will be perfect."

It's been a while since we've had a night just the two of us. Between preparing for the wedding and dividing my time between the salon and helping Graham's mom, we really haven't had a lot of extra time to hang out.

"That sounds like exactly what I need," Kinsley sighs, as she picks up her phone, tossing it into her purse. "I miss my Halle girl and I feel like we have a lot to catch up on."

An hour later, we're sitting on the couch with empty boxes of Chinese takeout sitting on our coffee table like a buffet. My hair is wrapped in a towel on the top of my head as Kinsley digs through her basket of nail polish trying to decide on the perfect color.

"I'm so full," I say, sighing as I lean back, patting my full and happy stomach.

"It was really good. I just can't eat very much right now," she replies. She flashes me a sad smile, before continuing to rummage through her polishes.

There are so many attractive colors, it's no wonder she's having a hard time deciding.

"Kins, I am sure you don't have anything to worry about. Wes loves you. He has since we were sixteen years old when he asked to take you to homecoming and you agreed, but only under the condition that he let you clean his locker."

I can't help but laugh thinking back on that memory because it's totally something she would say.

Looking up at me, she glares at me. "You know what you can do? Pick up those empty cartons."

I want to laugh, make a joke to pull her out of it, but I drop it. Picking up the garbage, I carry it into the kitchen. I make a pit stop by the bathroom, dropping off my wet towel and grabbing my comb to brush through my damp hair.

My phone vibrates with a text, seeing Graham's name flash on my screen.

Graham: You'll be on my mind all night. Have fun with Kins. Tell her I said hi.

Plopping back down on the couch next to Kinsley, I say, "Graham says hi."

Looking up at me, she smiles. It's the first real smile I've seen on her face all day. Running the comb through my hair, I flip through Netflix trying to find an episode of Friends that will help pull my friend out of her somber mood.

"How are things after the wedding?"

I think about her question for a minute while scrolling through episodes.

"Honestly, I guess I don't know. He apologized for leaving and for hurting me. I'm not sure where we go now though."

Even though we've talked every day since the wedding, I still don't know what's going on or what the future has in store for us.

"He loves you, Halle. I really think he regrets leaving you, for hurting you how he did. It was never supposed to be this way for you guys."

"I know he does."

Kinsley settles on a bright pink nail polish, setting the rest in the basket on the floor. Pressing play, we both settle in as the theme to Friends floats from the speakers.

"I think I just worry about it happening again, you know? What's stopping him from leaving Arbor Creek again? If I wasn't a reason for him to stay before, I don't trust he won't find a reason to go if something happens down the road."

"Who are you right now?" Her question throws me off, as I look over at her. She slips the brush back into the nail polish, setting it on the coffee table. She has this stern look on her face and it's throwing me off.

"The Halle I know is fearless. She doesn't get hung up on the what-ifs. She puts her all into everything. It's what I love about you. Don't let your fears hold you back from moving on with him."

"It's not that easy."

"I didn't say it was easy, Halle. Just promise me you'll give him a real chance."

"Okay, under one condition," I say, looking at her firmly.

"Shoot."

"Promise me you will have an actual conversation with Wes before you go assuming things."

She lets out a heavy sigh, picking up her nail polish again untwisting the cap.

"Kinsley Lea," I say, sounding like her mom.

"Will you stop that?" She laughs.

"I'm serious."

"I know you are, okay?" she sighs again before nodding her head. "I promise."

Reaching my pinky out between us like we've done since we were in middle school, she curls her finger around mine.

"If all else fails, we can live together until we're ninety-five. We can collect cats and cut coupons, and every Sunday we can go to the casino to play bingo."

"Sounds like a plan." I giggle. "Who needs sex when you can live off the high of gambling?"

chapter eighteen

GRAHAM

Pulling into a parking spot outside of Brodie's, I turn the key in the ignition and grab my phone just as it dings with a text message. Jumping out of my pickup, I hit the lock as I swipe the screen checking the message.

Halle: Remember that one time we locked ourselves out of my house?

Chuckling to myself, I think back to the night Halle and I had been hanging out. It was a Friday night and her parents were out of town. She had told her parents she was going to stay with Kinsley that night, but like every Friday night, we all met up for the game and then went out with our friends.

Halle had left her key in her house, but we had been desperate to spend time alone together. She had practically begged me to help her get inside. Like every other time, I couldn't deny her. I still remember hoisting her up to her bedroom window and the sarcastic comments she made about me touching her butt.

Graham: I'll never forget it. I'll never forget how great your ass looked in those jeans either.

Halle: You better not!

I can't help but chuckle. Pulling on the back door to Brodie's, it's a quiet crowd for lunch on a Friday. People are seated at the bar, starting their weekend early with a beer in their hand.

Spotting Mason, Brannon, and Wes at a table off to the side, I give a quick wave to Brea who's working at the bar, as I head toward them.

"We weren't sure if you were going to be able to make it," Brannon says, as he waves me over.

Sliding into the booth next to Mason, I reach over shaking each of their hands in greeting as I feel the stress of the day ease just a little.

Truth be told, I needed to get out of the office for a little bit and meeting up with the guys seems like the perfect way to do it. We haven't seen each other since the wedding and things were crazy, we haven't really had a chance to catch up.

"How are things going at the office?" Mason asks, looking over at me. "Dean mentioned shit has been tense lately with Krate coming around. What the hell's going on?"

Running my hand over my face, I settle into my seat resting my arm along the back. Glancing around, I make sure no one is around that could overhear our conversation before I look back at Wes wanting to ensure he's hearing this.

"He's been coming around Halle when she's alone, saying shit to her. It's freaking her out. She plays it off like it's not a big deal, like she can handle it herself, but I know better. It's evident how uncomfortable he makes her."

"You're shittin' me?" Brannon asks, resting his forearms on the table. He can play it off like he's the jokester, but I know he feels the same way I do. You don't treat a woman that way. You don't put that kind of fear in her.

"Nah, man, I wish I was though. We've been trailing him." I pause, adjusting myself in my seat again.

"Mav and I have been working with some people, keeping an eye on shit. He's just a loose cannon, unpredictable. He cornered her the other day outside Hudson's, middle of the damn day. He knows we're onto him, told her if I didn't stay away and mind my own business, he'd put me six feet under next to Gage."

I feel Mason freeze next to me.

"Hell, no," Brannon says, balling his hands up into a fist. "He's sayin' shit to her like that, there's no way she's doing okay."

"Yeah, I know. She's stubborn as a bull though." I emit an exhaustive sigh while running my hand across the back of my neck. I've tried going by after I found out what happened, but she denied me. I tried talking to her about it at the wedding, but she insists she's fine.

"I don't think he'd do anything to Kinsley. He's targeting me, but you know they're always together."

Wes nods his head, obviously not liking this. "Kinsley have any idea this is going on? She hasn't mentioned anything to me."

"I'm not sure, man. It's hard enough getting Halle to talk to me about it. She swears she's okay, but every time I bring it up, she changes the subject. She turns it around, about how she isn't going to turn to me if something's bothering her. I fucked up in the past and she is being stubborn about letting me be there for her again."

Wes's eyebrows furrow as he leans forward, rubbing his thumb over his lips in thought.

"Honestly, we haven't talked much this week." He squints, as he runs his palms over his weary eyes. "Brannon and I have been so busy with the motocross event coming into town. I was contracted to do some work on a bike to help get it ready. I had to cancel on our plans on Wednesday because of it. She wasn't happy with me about it. We just have both been so busy between Callum and Ellie's wedding and things taking off at the shop."

This is the first time I've ever heard of them having problems and I can sense it isn't sitting right with Wes either.

"I was thinking about taking her out of town for the weekend now that things will start calming down a little."

"You know, if you guys want to take off, I have no problem taking care of things for a bit. Hell, we all know I ain't got nothin' or no one waitin' on me at home," Brannon comments with a glint of humor.

"You sure about that?" Mason asks, laughing as he leans back against the back of the booth, shooting Brannon a look.

Yeah, we all saw how Brannon and Lissa were the night at Velvet in Chicago. As much as she can try to act like she's not interested, I know full well it's all a ploy. He loves getting under her skin and she loves throwing it right back at him.

"I don't know what you're talking about." Brannon gives him a side grin.

I laugh. That's like saying Halle and I kept our hands to ourselves that night too.

Brea picks the perfect moment to step up to our table.

"Sorry, I'm the only one running the bar and taking lunch orders. Danny called in today. You guys ready to order?" Brea asks, taking her notepad out from the front of her apron.

"I forgive you." Mason winks.

I lean back, feeling stuck in the middle of their sexual tension. I had enough of that rooming with him and living with them when I first moved back home before my house was ready. Hanging out with them when they were friends was great. Now they are in this new relationship and living together. It had reminded me all too much about what Halle and I used to have.

We spend the next hour talking with Wes about his weekend plans with Kinsley, while listening to Brannon's endless questioning of Brea as he presses for news on when Lissa will be coming to town to visit.

I have a feeling she'll be coming back to town very soon, if Brannon has anything to say about it.

After lunch wraps up, I decide to send a text to Halle. Knowing Kinsley will be taking off with Wes for the weekend, I hate the thought of Halle being alone at their place.

Graham: What do I have to do to see you tonight?

Climbing into my pickup, my phone dings with a response.

Halle: This sounds like it could be fun. I have a lot of ideas.

Graham: I sure do have my hands full with you, huh?

Halle: That's why you have two hands.

Chuckling, my chest warms picturing the smile on Halle's face as she typed out that response. This girl kills me.

Graham: Mm, that I do. Now I'm just thinking of all the things I can do with these hands.

Halle: Now this is what I'm talking about. Tell me more...

Graham: I want to know if any of your ideas include me re-learning all the ways your body can come alive under my touch.

The rumbling sound of an exhaust approaching draws my attention away from our conversation to my rearview mirror. As I glance up, I see Krate driving while rolling down his window.

Peering into the side mirror, our eyes lock on each other's. My phone rings in my hand, as he speeds off down the road.

"You still over at Brodie's?" Maverick asks, not even bothering with a greeting. He's been tailing him.

"Yep, he just pulled up right behind me."

"Motherfucker," Maverick swears.

Holding the phone up to my ear, I peer over my shoulder seeing him hit the gas as he guns it toward the back of the parking lot taking a sharp turn toward the alley.

"I was able to place the GPS last night. I know he's onto us, so I've eased up on him. At least until we can figure out what he and Hendrich are up to. Something's going down and he's trying to distract us with his bullshit."

He's right. He knows we've been watching him and he's trying to draw us to steer our focus in a different direction, away from whatever is going on.

"Alright, keep me updated. I don't trust this prick."

My phone pings with another text from Halle. Knowing Krate has shit up his sleeve and Halle is about to be staying at her place alone, I need to figure out a way to convince her to stay with me this weekend.

If I tell her the truth, I'm not sure how she'll take it. She may get pissed and likely tell me not to worry about it. The hell if I'll listen to that bullshit. She's my number one priority, her and my mom. I'm not about to let anything happen to either of them.

"I'm going to swing by Halle's salon and see if I can convince her to stay with me this weekend. Wes and Kinsley are going to be heading out of town, and I just don't feel good about her being alone."

I know Maverick understands. I'm already out of the parking lot and down main street toward her salon when he replies.

"Good luck," he mutters, knowing I'm going to have my hands full trying to convince her of that. We say our goodbyes and I let him know I'll be in touch with him.

Pulling into the alley behind her salon, I cut the engine when I spot her car in the parking lot. I don't see Kinsley's Jeep, so I'm immediately on alert thinking about her being alone.

The doorbell rings as I enter, and my eyes immediately fall on Halle. It's as if all my fears fall away when I see her beautiful smile lighting up her face.

There's an older woman I don't recognize sitting in front of her.

"Hey." She grins at me in the mirror. "Wasn't expecting you to show up. I'm almost done. If you want to take a seat at Kinsley's station, I'll be with you in a few."

She shoots me a wink as she resumes what she was doing, running her fingers through the woman's curled hair as she talks about some hair product she has in her other hand.

After the lady has paid and thanked Halle, she's out the door, and Halle's attention is turned back on me. Just where I want it.

"You didn't respond back to me. I didn't think it meant you were going to come waltzing through the door instead."

"Well, I thought if I was going to convince you to see me, the best way to do it would be standing in front of you. I thought there'd be less of a chance you'd say no."

She raises her eyebrow at me, knowingly.

"Is that your way of saying you know I can't turn you down when you're here tempting me." The edge of her mouth curves in a smile.

"You've practically admitted it. What do you have going on that's better than spending the weekend with me?"

"Oh, so now it's the weekend? Are you sure you're ready for that much time together? Be careful, Graham, you may find it difficult not to fall back in love with me."

"I was in trouble a long time ago."

chapter nineteen

HALLE

As we pull onto a gravel road on the outskirts of town, I am remembering the conversation Graham had with Mason and Callum on our drive back home from Chicago. Callum had been telling him about the process of building his house before he and Ellie had met.

I had been hesitant to believe he was going to be moving home to Iowa to stay for good. As Graham pulls up the drive leading to his house, I glance out the window taking in the large structure. The combination of dark brick and light wood gives it a rustic farmhouse feel. I bite my lip, using the back of my hand to hide the smile currently taking over my face.

I can feel Graham's eyes on me, waiting for some sort of reaction. I do my best to give nothing away as he pulls to a stop in front of the garage.

"What do you think?" he asks, reaching forward to put the gear in park, turning the ignition off.

"Wow, Graham," I say, sitting forward to look out the window. It's really the best I can come up with in this moment. My eyes are wide, as I peer over at him. "This is your house?"

"It is." He grins back at me. "Does that mean you like it?"

I want to laugh and for a second, I wonder why it matters if I like it, before I quickly let that go. Clutching the door handle, I pop open the door and climb out of the truck.

The gravel crunches beneath his feet as he walks around the front of the pickup, holding his hand out to me. Wrapping our fingers together, he leads me up the walkway to the front door.

It seriously looks like it's something out of a Better Homes and Gardens magazine or off the set of Fixer Upper. I'm kind of amazed for a bachelor pad, he's put this much thought and effort into his home.

He unlocks and pushes the door open, holding his hand out letting me lead the way.

Stepping one foot into the entryway, I feel like I'm once again struck speechless as I glance over my shoulder to look at Graham.

"Did you decorate this all yourself?"

He laughs, as if he was waiting for me to ask him this.

"I'm glad you like it," he answers.

Stepping down into the living area, I run my hand along the stone of the fireplace to the light oak mantel that hangs just above my shoulder. My eyes take in the rest of the room, to the dining area with the large table to the off white and black iron kitchen. It's nice, but the little touches like the box of car parts sitting on the chair in the dining room make it clear there's still a man living here.

"It's really nice, Graham. I love it. I bet it's really peaceful out here too," I say, walking through the dining room to peer out the sliding glass door overlooking the backyard.

"Yeah, it's quiet but that's how I like it."

He walks up behind me. Even if I couldn't see his reflection in the window, I could still feel his presence around me. The warmth of this body heat radiates off him and onto my back, as he steps closer.

We're like two magnets, unable to resist the pull between us. Leaning back, I rest my head against his shoulder. His arms wrap around my middle, pulling me closer to him and for a moment I let everything else fall away. I soak in this moment and let myself enjoy having him here. I let myself think about us together again and maybe one day living together here in this beautiful home.

"It's so good to have you here," he whispers, pressing a kiss against my shoulder.

My breath gets caught in my throat at the tingles that spread across my skin feeling his mouth on me again. I tilt my head to the side, giving him better access and the moan that emanates from his chest tells me he appreciates it.

My head rolls across his chest as my fingers dig into his forearms, holding him closer to me. He moves, pressing his body closer, and I can't help but let a moan escape me, too, when I feel his hard length press against the curve of my ass.

His tongue traces a line from the base of my neck up the column just below my ear. His warm breath against the trail of wetness he left in his wake.

My body quivers beneath his touch, as Graham's hands slip under the cotton of my tank top, pressing against my stomach.

"You look so fucking beautiful," he groans, tilting his head up. "Look at you, Halle."

Opening my eyes, it takes a moment for them to adjust to the light. The light from the kitchen shining behind us makes the darkness that's now fallen outside the perfect backdrop highlighting our reflection.

His hand slides down, as his fingers brush across the button of my denim jeans. I'm not sure if he's thinking what I'm thinking, but I want to beg him to keep going.

His fingers dip just below my waistband, touching the lace edge of my panties.

"Lace," he mutters, as he bites down against the curve of my neck to stifle his moan. He doesn't do it hard, but feeling his moan vibrate against my skin has me pressing my ass against him wanting to drive him wilder.

His hand, however, doesn't stop its exploration. Pushing the button through, he lowers the zipper of my pants and with little effort, the denim falls to the floor at my feet.

"Mm," he hums his appreciation, as he stares hungrily at me in the window.

"Graham," I say, my words coming out breathy with each heavy rise and fall of my chest.

"Yes, baby," he says, trailing kisses down my neck to where the strap of my tank top sits. He uses his free hand to pull the strap down, giving him better access to my skin as he continues his path.

He stops, grabbing the hem of my shirt as he pulls the material over my head. When he sees the lace of my strapless bra, I know this is it.

"Dear God," he mutters, as he drops to his knees behind me. He kisses, licks, and nips the skin from the back of my knee up my thigh to the curve of my ass.

My hand reaches blindly behind me, grabbing his hair, holding him to me. He growls back, loving my nails against his scalp, as he gently bites my backside.

His hands grab my hips, turning me to face him as he presses his forehead against my stomach just before he continues the same path he had made before from my knee, up my inner thigh, stopping as he presses his lips against my lace covered pussy.

His warm breath over my heated skin is nearly my undoing. My fingers grab his hair roughly, holding him closer to me. His tongue darts out, wetting the material and I feel his body shake against me.

We're both sitting on the edge, need consuming every inch of our bodies, but we hold back not wanting to give into it just yet.

Graham tilts his head back. Seeing his eyes bright, glossed over with how turned on he is makes me want to beg him to keep going.

"Stay with me," he says. My brows furrow in confusion. Of all the things I expected for him to say in this moment, that isn't the one I thought I'd hear.

"You mean tonight?" I say, confused for a second if I understood him correctly.

"Yes, tonight. Or this weekend, why not keep these good times going?" He winks. I want to laugh at his smirk, as my fingers dig into his hair again.

"Can't we talk about this after?"

"Oh, so you want me to keep going?"

My eyes bug out of my head at the audacity of him. He's playing it cool, like he's oblivious to the way my body is practically shaking with need.

He sits back on his haunches. He's waiting for me to scold him, beg him, anything to stop this conversation and go back to the sweet torture he was inflicting upon me just a few moments ago.

"I'm hungry," he says, clapping his hands together as he looks back up at me. "How about you? Are you hungry?"

Then he winks at me again. The motherfucker has the audacity to wink at me when I want nothing more than to grab him by his hair and put his mouth back on me, making him shut up.

"Graham," I say, grinding my teeth.

He's loving this, and I want to stomp my feet and command him to stop. He pushes to his feet, reaches for the chair at the head of the table, and takes a seat as he looks over at me. He reaches his hand out to me and I place mine in his, just before he yanks me closer to him.

His hands wrap around my waist as he moves me so I'm standing between his legs, positioning me between him and the edge of the table.

"Mm, yes. I'm very, very hungry."

He looks up at me and my breath is caught in my throat at the hunger I see in his eyes. I realize then he's not at all talking about serving me a three-course meal.

No, it's the furthest thing from his mind and I want to yell *hallelujah.*

He picks me up and sets me on the edge of the table, as he commands me to lie back. This is a new side of Graham that I've never seen.

He's always wanted to take care of me, pleasure me, but the edge of authority in his voice is so fucking hot. I want more of it, so I do as he says and lie back.

My heels are both positioned at the edge of the table. Peering down, I watch as Graham stands. He's like a man on a mission, as he wraps his fingers around the lace of my underwear, whispering for me to lift as he pulls them over my hips and down my legs.

I force my knees together, as if trying to hold onto some sense of modesty, as he sits back down in the seat. When I feel his rough hands on the soft skin of my thighs, all thoughts of modesty go right out the window, wanting to feel whatever he's willing to give me.

I hear him moan in appreciation, as I squeeze my eyes closed just before his tongue swipes at my entrance. The sensations cause my body to tremble, as I reach down to run my fingers through his hair, holding him against me.

Raising my head up, I peer down my body at him as his eyes look up to meet mine. His lips wrap around my clit, sucking as my legs clutch against the side of his face.

"Oh, God, Graham," I cry, holding his head to me.

My body thrashes back and forth, as he wraps his hands around my thighs holding them close to him. He growls, it's loud and animalistic. The sound vibrates through my body.

He pulls back, away from me, using his finger to run through my wetness down to my pussy. When it slowly slides inside of me, I want to beg him to give me more, and sensing what I need, he does. He leans forward again, using a combination of his tongue and his finger to bring me closer and closer to the edge.

He alternates between licking and sucking. Each move is unexpected, and it's exactly what I love. Tingles break out across my skin as I squeeze my eyes shut. Lights flash before my eyes as I let out a soft moan and shivers rack through my body.

I should feel embarrassed, the way I'm laid out before Graham. It dawns on me that up until now, it's always been about me. Him taking care of me and pleasuring me.

I want to take care of him in the same way.

He stands up, peering down at me. Somewhere along the way he shed his shirt, which is now laying on the floor behind him. I can't help but smile thinking about him quickly taking it off and throwing it haphazardly out of the way.

"My turn," I say, raising my eyebrows at him suggestively.

His eyes light up at me, running his hands along my thighs as he reaches forward pressing a kiss there.

"Is that so?"

"Mhmm." I smile, content.

"Does that mean you're going to stay with me?"

The thought of lying in bed with Graham, being wrapped up in his arms all night after spending the past five years going to bed thinking about him, missing him, sounds more like a dream than reality. As much as I should pump the brakes, hold myself back, and ask him what's going on, I also don't want to stop and question things either. I don't want to make things complicated and I sure as hell don't want to ruin this moment right now between us.

"I guess," I say, smiling at him. He tilts his head back as I lean forward pressing a kiss against his lips. I can taste myself on him. I wrap my hand around the side of his face, feeling the stubble lining his jaw against my hand.

"You're mine," he mutters against my mouth. "All. Night. Long." Each word is followed by a kiss against my lips.

The sound of vibration against the hardwood floor distracts us from the happy bubble we have around us. He reaches over, grabbing it, and checks the screen before looking back at me.

He sighs deeply as he stands looking at me regretfully.

"I'm sorry. I gotta take this." He holds the phone up to me, just as he swipes the screen.

"What's up?" he asks, pressing the phone against his ear.

I watch as he disappears into the living room. His words are muffled, so I'm not able to make out the conversation. There's a part of me that wonders what could be so important it's worth answering right now. I quickly force that thought out of my mind. He owns his own company now, there could be a hundred more important things going on he has to tend to.

I feel selfish for letting my mind go there. I just hate that our moment was ruined.

On shaky legs, I climb off the table and quickly put my clothes back on. We have a whole night ahead of ourselves now and I tell myself I'm going to enjoy this time with him, because I know all too well how quickly it can be taken away from me.

I'm going to make this night count.

chapter twenty

GRAHAM

Two hands wrap low around my waist while I'm standing shirtless in the kitchen.

"You know it's dangerous to cook without a shirt on," she mumbles from behind me, pressing her lips against my spine as her fingers trail along the edge of my sweatpants down to brush over my cock.

I set the spatula on the counter and turn in her arms to face her. Her hair is wet, piled in a messy thing on her head. Her face is clean, and my God she looks so damn beautiful. I love seeing her making herself at home here.

"I remember how very skilled you are in this kitchen," she says, hinting at our time together on the oak table just a few feet away.

She presses a kiss against my chest, peering up at me with an arch in her brow.

"You are trouble," I mutter, grabbing her so my hands frame her face as I kiss her lips roughly. "You're more dangerous to me than you realize. I'd do anything for you. Absolutely anything, without care of the consequences or the repercussions. You make me reckless, Halle."

Her eyes brighten, with a hint of a sparkle to them. She runs her teeth over her bottom lip and it takes all the focus I have left out of me. I want to wrap her in my arms, kiss her and take over biting that lip.

"Mm," she moans, kissing a path over my chest. She drags her nails over my hips, along the waistband of my pants.

"Have I told you how fucking sexy you look in sweatpants?"

Raising my brow at her, I fold my arms in front of me. Her eyes trail over my chest, over my abs, to take in my pants. "Is that so?"

"You're like sinful eye candy. You're lucky I'd let you out of the house wearing those, much less the bedroom."

She shakes her head, turning to grab two glasses from the cabinet setting them on the counter. She must pick up on my confusion as she turns, closing the distance between us once again.

She's no more than a couple inches from me when she stops. I feel the heat radiating off her as she looks down between us, before her eyes meet mine once again. Her small hand reaches out, running over my cock, as I suck in a breath.

"Halle," I respond sternly, warning her.

"I can see the outline of your dick in your pants, Graham," she replies with the same firm tone. She leans forward, closing the distance between us, but her grip never loosens.

"I'm thirsty," she says, smiling as she turns and pads over to the fridge just a few feet away.

She's getting me back after how I played with her.

"Fucking trouble," I groan.

The pan sizzles behind me forcing my attention away. I curse, seeing the smoke coming from the pan of eggs I had been cooking up until she came in here distracting me.

"My bad," she jokes, as she opens the fridge door, grabbing the orange juice.

The eggs are dunzo, so I quickly scrape them off into the garbage and then crack two more in the pan starting over from scratch.

"We're never going to eat if you keep that up. How about you stay over there for now?"

"Where's the fun in that?" She giggles, pouring a glass of juice as she takes a seat on the counter facing me.

"There's no fun," I joke, looking at her legs in her yoga pants. They fit her like a fucking glove, leaving little to the imagination. I remember how great she looked just a few hours ago when she was sitting on the edge of the table. She must realize where my mind has drifted, as I mutter a quiet "fuck" turning my focus back on the eggs.

After a couple minutes go by, I attempt to change the subject. "I was thinking, I need to stop by my mom's house today to get some yard work done. If you don't have any plans, I'd love for you to join me. I know she'd be happy to see you too."

"I thought I was yours all weekend. Tell me where you want me and I'm there."

Turning to glance over my shoulder, I watch as she bites her lip again as she raises the glass of juice to her mouth. Pausing, I watch the way her throat swallows it down before my eyes find hers again.

When she sets the glass down on the counter, she does little to hide the smirk on her face.

Narrowing my eyes at her, I shake my head as I turn my attention back on the food.

"You're damn right you are," I respond, as I mutter "trouble" under my breath. I can hear her muffled laugh behind me, as I smile a grin of my own.

Later that morning, Halle and I stop by her place to feed her cat before we head over to my mom's. She's been feeling better over the past week, so she is up doing some things around the house when we get there.

"Well, isn't this a wonderful surprise. I wasn't expecting both of you today," my mom exclaims, turning around from where she stands doing the dishes in the kitchen.

"We thought we'd come over and help you. I was thinking I could make you lunch while Graham gets all dirty outside," Halle says, pulling my mom in for a hug.

"You are too sweet. You don't have to do that," she replies, hugging her back.

"Of course, I don't have to." Halle smiles, winking at me. "I want to though. You hungry for anything in particular?"

I smile watching how Halle makes herself at home, sliding up next to my mom as she takes a clean towel off the counter and begins drying off the dishes. I watch them both together as Halle talks to her about some TV show they both are into watching. I've heard of it but have no idea what they are talking about as they get into naming all these women at something called a rose ceremony.

I excuse myself as I head out to the shed behind the house and unload the mower. Popping in my ear-buds, I get to work on mowing the yard. The summer sun is blazing, leaving sweat dripping down my forehead. It's been a while since we've had any rain, but I sense a storm will be rolling through soon. The humidity is so thick, the moment you walk out the door it feels like a brick wall of hot air nearly taking your breath away.

"I thought you could use a glass of water," Halle says a little while later.

Wiping the sweat dripping off my brow, I cut the engine on the weedwhacker. Setting it down in the grass, I turn and take a step closer to her. Chugging the water, I appreciate the bite from the cool liquid as I swallow it down.

"Ahh, that was great. Thank you." I lean forward to give Halle a kiss.

She tilts her head back, away from me, eyeing the sweat that's dripping down from my hair onto my chest.

"You're a little sweaty." She giggles.

"A little sweat never bothered you before," I retort, raising my brow. "In fact, just last night you seemed almost enthusiastic over how hard I was working."

Setting the plastic cup on the railing of the wood deck, I turn toward Halle raising my eyebrows suggestively to her. She knows what's coming, as she hurries backward in an attempt to flee.

"Oh, now she runs away. Just this morning you were rubbing that sexy body all over me, egging me on, but now a little sweat has you running."

"Graham, you look like you just jumped in a pool," she begs, holding her hand up between us as if that's going to stop me.

Stalking toward her, a grin breaks out across her face as she bolts away from me around the tree.

"Don't you dare do it, or I swear," she warns, peeking at me from behind the tree. She has a seriousness in her eye, but I'm not falling for it.

"Or what, Halle? What are you going to do?" I jest.

"No sex," she spits out frantically.

I laugh because the moment she says it, her face looks like she wishes she could take it back.

"No sex, huh? You think you'll be able to hold out long enough to punish me? How long you think you'd be able to make it? A day, maybe two?"

She narrows her eyes at me, stepping out from behind the tree. Her hands are planted firmly on her hips, clearly not amused.

"Are you mocking me?"

"Me? Mock you?" I laugh, holding my hand up against my chest. "I wouldn't dare."

She huffs at the sight of my smirk.

"C'mon, Halle, just let me give you a kiss. A little sweat now will make up for the misery you'd be putting yourself through later," I joke.

I take a step toward her, then another. I get a foot away from her before she attempts to bolt again. Reaching out, I grab her by her arm and pull her back to me.

"Oh, Graham, you're wet," she cries, her back pressed against my chest as I lean forward kissing her neck.

"Oh my God, you're so gross." She laughs, feigning that she's mad and hates it but the giggles that ensue tell a different story.

"Don't try to run from me again, Halle Keegan. I let you go once, I'm not going to let it happen again," I growl, kissing her neck.

"Promise?"

"You're damn right I promise. I'm never letting you go."

Wrapping my arms like a band around her waist, I hold her close to me and she melts into me at those words.

"You're lucky I like you," she whispers, and I moan in appreciation.

She turns in my arms, giving into me and finally letting me kiss her. We are lost in our own world, like we always are, when Halle breaks her lips apart taking a step away from me.

"Do you smell that?" She looks frantic, looking over at the house scanning across the yard, then back to me.

"Smell what?"

"You don't smell that?" she asks, looking concerned. "It smells like something's burning."

The words are no more out of her mouth when the sound of an explosion hits. Flames erupt toward the side of the garage.

Panic surges through me, quickly replaced with adrenaline. I hear Halle cry my name, as I run over toward where the fire hits.

"Halle, I need you to get my mom out of the house. Now. Hurry."

Halle races over to the deck and up the stairs. "Call 911!" I yell, as she disappears inside.

Flames burst from the garbage cans sitting along the side of the garage. Thankfully I already had the hose out, watering the flowers in the backyard. Grabbing it from where it lies on the ground, I spray water on the fire, doing everything I can to stop it from spreading. I just want Halle and my mom to get out of there.

"Graham, they're coming!" Halle shouts, standing in the street. I see my mom across the street in our neighbors' yard, her hand covering her mouth.

The tightness in my chest eases seeing they are both safe as sirens blare, approaching.

It all happens so quickly. Firefighters, police officers, and EMT workers show up.

Just like that, I'm pulled back to the night of Gage's accident as I run across the street, wrapping my mom and Halle in a hug. Watching as they furiously work to put out the fire, I picture the red and blue lights flashing in my face that night. The same burning sensation in my lungs as I struggled through every breath.

I whisper in my mom's ear that I love her and pull Halle in a hug pressing a kiss against her temple. Our earlier banter is gone, as she wraps her arms around me holding me against her. Her body trembles in my arms, the adrenaline we both feel running high. I rub my hand over her back, reassuring her it's okay.

I'm reminded how life can change in a moment's notice. Holding the two women I love more than anything close to me, I vow once again to myself and to God, I will give my last breath before I'd ever let anything happen to them.

chapter twenty-one

HALLE

Graham: *Got plans tonight? Thinking about hitting up the races with the guys. Wanna join? Wes is gonna talk to Kins about coming too.*

A smile breaks out across my face at the thought of seeing him. We used to go to the races all the time growing up. In fact, we all thought Wes was going to be the next big star to hit motocross until he injured his back right after high school. It was devastating to him, something I think still bothers him to this day.

I shoot back a text telling him I'm there and he replies saying to be ready in thirty minutes. I check the clock, seeing it's already after six. It's crazy how fast the day has flown by. Although I feel like I've been milling around in a cloud since I got home.

Spending the weekend with Graham was totally unexpected but meant everything to me. Although I still haven't been able to get my mind off the fire at his mom's house. I keep thinking about what could've happened had we not been there. What if it would've spread to her house and she didn't know it until it was too late?

I shake myself from my thoughts, pressing my fingers against my forehead massaging them.

"You okay?" Kinsley asks, catching me off guard.

"Yeah, just thinking about how bad the fire at Sandy's house could've been had we not been there."

"Oh, yeah," she says, bending her knee on the edge of my bed. The look on her face matches mine. She understands the worry I feel thinking about all Sandy's been through and now to add this to the situation.

"I'm sure it's okay. I mean, really, who would try to do something to Sandy? She's the sweetest woman in town. I'm sure after they investigate it, everything will be fine."

"Yeah, I'm sure you're right," I sigh, walking over to my closet looking for a change of clothes.

"Wes just texted me about heading down to the track to watch the races. He mentioned you and Graham are coming with." She smiles. I know she's loving how much time we're spending together, but even more that we're all now doing things together again.

"Yeah, he said he's going to be here to pick me up in a bit."

Clapping her hands together, she jumps to her feet. "Yay, that makes me so happy."

She bounces around the room gleefully, pausing to check herself out in the mirror.

"I'm going to change quick and head over to Wes's to meet up with him. We'll see you down there shortly then." She reaches up and starts gathering her long dark hair into a ponytail. She checks her reflection as she ties her hair back, before she pecks a kiss against my cheek and flounces out the door.

I spend the next few minutes busying myself with getting ready too. The warm August sun will start to set here soon. When the sun goes down and the night sky takes over, it will get chilly. I grab a hoodie out of my closet and opt for a fitted T-shirt, denim shorts, and my Chucks.

After spending a few minutes styling my hair in a messy bun, I'm right on time when I hear the doorbell ringing. I don't bother checking who it is, as I swing the door open and smile up at Graham.

The look on his face is all serious and I realize my error in that exact moment. I almost want to slam the door in his face and do it all over again.

"Halle," he growls.

"Whoops." I lock my jaw, forcing a smile through gritted teeth.

"What did I tell you about checking who it is before you just swing the door open? What if it wasn't me?"

"I knew it was you." I grin, wrapping my hand into the front of his shirt and pulling him inside.

I wrap my hands around his waist, holding him close to me as I press my face against his chest. At the risk of looking like a total weirdo, I take a deep breath and inhale him in. He smells so good. Woodsy, like he just spent the afternoon in a forest cutting down trees.

His strong arms surround me, and I just want to get lost in the feeling of being close to him. You'd think it's been months, not just a few hours, since we stood exactly like this. I don't know if I'll ever get enough of him after being apart for so long.

"I missed you," he whispers against the side of my head and I don't hold back the grin that takes over my face.

It's like he was reading my thoughts, knowing how much I missed being away from him.

"I missed you." I smile, tilting my head back so I can stare at him.

He winks at me, pressing a kiss against my mouth. Running my palms over his firm chest, I wrap my hand around the base of his neck and hold him to me. When his tongue brushes along my lower lip, seeking entrance, I don't even hesitate to let him in.

And just like that I'm lost in this moment with him again. When our lips break apart, we stand here with his forehead pressed against mine as we both work to regain our breath.

"How was your day?"

I wait for him to answer, all while thinking about how crazy I'll probably look to him when I tell him how I literally couldn't keep my mind off him all day. How I was tuning out my clients when they talked, thinking back about our time in the dining room followed by our long night together in his bed.

"Busy," he says, running the palms of his hands over his eyes. The fatigue I noticed the night of the wedding is still there. It hurts a little thinking about how different his day probably was for him.

"What's wrong?"

"Just a lot going on at the office. Then, the fire chief stopped by to talk to me about the fire at my mom's."

The mention of the fire piques my interest, as I pull him behind me into the living room. I urge him to sit down beside me on the couch, taking his hand waiting to hear what he says next.

Not liking the way we're seated, he scoots back and picks up my legs so they're laying across his lap before wrapping his hands back around mine. I rest my head on his shoulder, as I wait for him to continue.

"They confirmed it was arson," he sighs.

Sitting up, I look at him. I know they were going to investigate it, and despite the worry in the back of my mind, I still expected them to come back with a different answer.

"Do they have any suspects?" Immediately my mind jumps back to our conversation about Krate and what he told me the other night. I imagine someone trying to hurt Sandy and it kills me to think about the extent they would be willing to go now to do so.

"They do," he says, pausing as he looks at me. "Apparently they think it's some kid who lives nearby. He was caught doing the same thing last month at a house down behind Brodie's."

"Do you believe them?"

He looks over at me, and I see the answers in his eyes. This is what is wearing on him. He doesn't believe it for a second.

"Not at all. I can't help but think it has to do with Krate and his guys. After that night he bothered you outside of Hudson's, we think he's been trying to send a message for us to back off him. We know something is about to go down, we're just not sure what. He's trying to scare us into backing down."

"Graham," I say, confirming my earlier fears. What lengths are they willing to go to try and get them to back down?

"Halle, do you trust me to always keep you safe?"

Squeezing his hands in mine, I hold them up to my mouth as I press a kiss against his skin. He leans forward and presses a kiss against my lips. I want to get lost in him right now. I want to forget about the world outside my doorstep and just stay here, just the two of us, forever.

"Do you trust me?" he asks, as our lips break apart.

"You know I do," I whisper. I realize then that I do. Despite everything that happened between us before, I do believe he's always done right by me. We may not always agree on what that means, but I do believe he wants to keep me safe and protect me.

"Good, I need you to trust me right now. I would never let anything happen to you or my mom. I'd go down fighting, I'd give my very last breath before I'd ever let anyone hurt you."

Tears form in my eyes because even though I know without a doubt he means what he says, I hope it would never come to that.

He presses his hand against the side of my face, running his thumb underneath my eyes to catch a tear trailing down my cheek.

"Don't cry, baby. You're too beautiful to be crying."

"I'm sorry," I whisper, running the palms of my hands over my face. "I'm okay, I promise."

Taking a deep breath, I flash Graham a hesitant smile as he moves my legs to stand.

"C'mon, let's forget everything and go have some fun."

He holds his hands out in front of me and I grab them, as he pulls me to stand with him. As soon as I'm standing, he wraps his arms around me in a hug as he whispers "I promise" into my ear before grabbing my hand again and pulling me alongside him over to the front door.

The excitement I had felt earlier feels like it's been sucked right out of me.

"Do you think we should still go? What about your mom? Maybe we should go over and stay with her for a little bit."

"Halle, I promise you she's alright. I have eyes on her place right now. I need you to trust me," he whispers.

Hearing him mention he has eyes on her right now, my mind drifts to when I was outside Hudson's, the night I ran into Krate and how quickly it seemed like Maverick swooped in and ran him off.

I can't help but wonder if he has eyes on me too. He just promised he would go down fighting to protect us both and to keep us safe. It dawns on me there are times when we are not together, and I wonder if he's protecting me from a distance when that's the case.

"Now c'mon," he says, swatting at my butt as he winks at me. "Let's get moving."

My eyes narrow at him, challenging him which earns me a laugh. He's in for it alright.

Standing in the entryway, I prop my foot up on the bench and slip on my shoe, leaning forward to tie it.

Glancing over my shoulder at Graham, I watch the way he stares at me. His eyes eat up every inch of my lower body. He's always had a thing for my legs, that goes back to our days in high school.

Clearing my throat, his eyes dart up to mine and he realizes then he's been busted. He doesn't even argue how he was blatantly staring at me. Picking up my other shoe, I move to slip it on and bend forward once again to tie it.

"We're not going to get very far if you keep looking at me like that."

"Tell me, how exactly am I looking at you right now?"

"Like you want to bend me over this bench and forget every plan we had made for tonight."

Without a word, his body is pressed against my back, leaving little room between us as his arms band around me holding me to him. One hand is wrapped around my lower body, skating along the waist of my denim shorts while the other is draped over my chest, his palm holding the curve of my breast in his hand.

"Don't tempt me, Halle," he whispers in my ear, running his nose over my cheek before he presses a kiss there.

I know I'm challenging him, pushing him to follow through with his warning. Sticking my ass out farther, I rotate my hips just enough to rock back and forth over him. I bite my lip to keep from moaning when I feel how turned on he is already.

"God, you drive me fucking crazy."

He reaches up, grabbing my jaw in his hand as his other arm is still wrapped tightly around my waist. Moving my face to look at him, he presses a kiss hard against my mouth swallowing my groan.

I rub my ass against him again, wanting more. I whisper "c'mon" to him earning me another deep growl. I want to grin, loving his reaction to me. I think back to the other night and how he has continued to take care of me, pleasure me.

The thought of me on my knees in front of him, like he was with me, giving him every ounce of pleasure and hearing his moans in response to how I'm making him feel has my body breaking out in tingles.

I reach my hand out behind my back, flexing my hand around his steel length. He lets out a deep hiss and hearing how much it's driving him wild only urges me forward.

"You're tempting me," he grits out, as my hand continues to jack him through his denim pants.

"I know," I breathe out, tilting my head back onto his shoulder. The move gives him better access to my neck and he goes in for the attack sucking and nipping every inch of skin. I know without a doubt that he's leaving a mark and I love it.

His grip on me loosens and I move to turn so I'm facing him, adjusting my hand but never stopping the steady rhythm of my hand jerking him up and down.

"Halle," he warns, and I know he's telling me he's close.

I drop down to my knees in front of him. The move takes him by surprise, causing his eyes to widen and I can't help but smile gleefully at his reaction.

Undoing the button and sliding the zipper down, I wrap my fingers into his boxer briefs as I tug them forcefully down his legs freeing him from the confines of his pants. Dear God, he's a fucking sight to see, as his hard length bobs in front of me.

Wrapping my hand around him again, I circle my lips around the head and take him deep into my mouth. Feeling him bump against the back of my throat, I moan around him. The vibrations have him muttering out a curse, as his fingers wrap around my chin holding me close to him.

I add suction as I pull back before I force him deep in my throat again. I pick up the pace, keeping the same movement over and over. His fingers wrap around my head, but he's careful not to tangle them into my hair, as he moans repeatedly. Seeing how he reacts to me, how tight his body is wound up, I want to practically beg him to let me taste him.

I don't let up and I can tell he's close when he locks his legs and shouts my name. He's warning me again, only this time I know he's telling me he's close. I don't stop though, and he moans in appreciation, followed by a deep "fuuuck."

His body vibrate with release, as I hold onto his thighs. His hips piston in and out of my mouth, until they finally come to a stop. His legs almost give out as he moves to sit on the bench seat in front of me.

He leans forward, wrapping his hand around my chin, pressing a hard kiss against my mouth. Leaning back, I run my finger over my chin before sliding my finger into my mouth.

Graham watches me in awe, before he presses another deep kiss against my lips.

"You are trouble," he moans, kissing me again. "Fucking trouble."

I want to laugh because I feel like I'm right there with him.

chapter twenty-two

GRAHAM

The smell of exhaust permeates the air from the dirt bikes. We hear the announcer thanking everyone for coming out tonight, the sound of dirt bikes' engines revving in the background.

Wrapping my arm around Halle's shoulder, I pull her in closer to me. She tilts her head against my chest. Even with the noise around us, I can hear her sigh in contentment. I feel it with her.

With all the shit going on at work, the stress of Krate, and the fire at my mom's, being able to get away from everything and come back to a place that holds so many memories for us is very therapeutic.

"It's been so long since I've been here." There's a smile in her voice when she says it. All night we've been like this, holding each other, touching each other in little ways. We haven't spoken about what's going on between us. The last time we did, I reminded her painfully how it was best for her that we weren't together.

Although after that, it seemed like everything went out the window because my need to be near her and protect her wrapped around me like a vise. It put a lot of things into perspective for me.

Our friends seemed pleased to see us turning back to our old ways. While they knew that something was going on with us, up until that point we had held back on showing affection toward each other when they were around. When we were alone though, it was like nothing was off limits. We were the same couple, if not more affectionate, than we were back then.

"Nothing makes me feel like home more than being out at the track," I press my lips against the side of her head and finish, "with you."

She tilts her head back, looking at me, as we continue our walk toward her car. She insisted on driving, saying we always take my pickup, so I decided to indulge her a little.

Pressing a kiss against her lips, we round the back of her car as we approach the driver's side. Pushing her up against the door, I wrap my hands around her thighs and lift her up using the car to support her. Her legs wrap around my waist and I want to fall to my knees when I feel her warmth pressed against me.

"Dear God," I moan, diving in to kiss her neck.

The sun has gone down. The cool breeze is flowing through the wide-open space of the fields surrounding the dirt track.

Halle's fingers slide into my hair, holding me close to her. I can feel her swallow beneath my lips, her breathing picking up pace as I kiss along the column of her neck and over her jaw. Wrapping my hand around her chin, I hold her face and kiss her deeply earning me a soft moan.

"Do you know how hard it was not to do this back there? I've been dying to kiss you since we left your house," I groan, kissing along her jaw up to her ear. Rubbing my aching cock against her, I let her feel just how much I want her.

It's like something inside me has broken, all the restraint I once had is let free and I can't get enough of her.

"Want to come stay with me tonight?" I run my tongue over the shell of her ear, nipping her. I hear her shutter a breath, as her nails dig into my skin at the base of my neck.

"Yes," she breathes out. "Let's get going or I'm going to have you doing something that is considered against the law in this very parking lot."

Lowering her to the ground, I reach behind her to open the door as she slides into the seat. I flash her a wink before I shut the door behind her and race around to the other side.

The drive back takes us about fifteen minutes. We drive with my hand wrapped around her thigh, trailing my thumb over her soft skin. Luke Combs plays through the speakers and Halle chats animatedly about gossip she heard about Brannon and Brea's friend, Lissa. Lissa has been close-lipped about what happened between them when she was in town for Ellie and Callum's wedding.

"Graham," Halle says, her voice is serious this time catching me off guard. "I can't tell who it is, but I think the person behind us is following me."

The dark night sky makes it difficult to make out who's driving behind us. Holding onto the head rest of Halle's seat, I peer out the window over my shoulder.

"Do me a favor, baby, and make a few turns," I say, keeping my eyes focused on the car behind us.

She pulls onto the next road and sure enough, the car behind us follows along behind. A few seconds later, she makes a sharp turn onto another road essentially bringing us in a circle and once again the car is right behind us turning too.

"Graham," she mutters nervously. "What should I do?"

"Take another left up here and let's head back to the highway. Try to stop for a second before you turn. I want to try to see what kind of car it is."

"Okay," she responds. Her voice flutters with nervousness.

Rubbing my hand over her shoulder, I try to let her know I'm here. The tension in her shoulders ease just a little.

As soon as we roll to a stop, I'm able to make out just enough of the front hood to see the GTO emblem and I immediately know who it is.

"Son of a bitch," I curse out, slipping my phone out of my pocket and quickly dialing Maverick's number.

"What's up?" he answers, the sound of music blaring behind him.

"Where are you?"

"At Tattered with Ryan. What's going on?" Tattered is the tattoo shop his girlfriend, Ryan, co-owns.

"I'm with Halle, we're driving back from Big Nasty and we're being followed." I glance over at Halle, reaching to touch her thigh again. "It's Krate."

Halle's eyes flash to me, wide with worry before focusing back on the road. Her hands grip the wheel with so much force, her knuckles turn white.

"Where are you?" Mav asks. He tells his girlfriend, Ryan, he's gotta go and a few seconds later, the music disappears just before the exhaust on his pickup roars to life.

"We're coming down Highway 30. We're in Halle's car, heading to my place."

"Alright, I'm heading that way."

He cuts the line. Thankfully he'll be coming from Everton, so he will likely be coming up on us very soon.

"It's gonna be alright, baby. You're doing good," I reassure her, just as the loud rumbling of the engine behind us revs.

Krate drives up on us, nearly rear-ending Halle's car, before breaking and doing it again once more.

"Graham," she cries, her hands fisting the steering wheel as she picks up speed.

"Be careful, baby, you're doing great. We're almost home," I say.

We're still about seven minutes away. In this moment, I hate that I let her drive tonight. I wish I would've driven, and it was me in the driver's seat. Although I know if the roles were reversed, there's no way in hell that stupid son of a bitch would be playing this game with me.

Glancing out the side mirror, I notice a pickup truck come up on us and a moment later a honk ensues.

"Oh, God, what was that?"

"That's Maverick, baby. You're doing great. Pick up the speed just a little bit but be careful. I don't want you to get into an accident. I just want us to get home."

"Okay." She trembles, pressing on the gas.

My phone vibrates in my hand and I quickly swipe the screen, answering it.

"It's definitely Krate, that stupid son of a bitch!" Maverick shouts.

"Yeah, I know. He's been riding on our ass. Do me a favor and get rid of him. I want to get Halle home."

"You got it. Let me know when you make it home."

"Alright," I say, rubbing my hand along Halle's leg again hoping to reassure her.

I disconnect the call and turn my attention to my woman sitting next to me. All my biggest fears feel like they are about to become reality. Ever since the day I lost Gage, all I've thought about is what would happen if something happened to Halle or my mom. The fear of losing one of them, letting them down, has damn near crippled me.

Here I am in this moment, feeling like I'm out of control and could lose her, and I don't even know what to do.

"Baby, Mav is here and he's going to help us lose him. Okay? I need you to just focus on the road and getting us home. We're almost there, baby. Just get us home."

Maverick pulls his truck into the lane next to us, toward oncoming traffic and races up next to Krate as he revs his engine again before slamming on his brakes and swerving back behind him. He continues to run up behind him, riding on his ass warning him to let us go.

Distracting him long enough, Halle quickly swerves over into the right turning lane that veers off onto the gravel road leading to my house. Slowing enough to take the corner, I turn back to check if Krate is following us to see that he and Maverick continue to fly past us.

Halle lets out a heavy sigh as she pulls over to the side of the road.

"It's okay, baby." I lean over and kiss her, as she puts it into park and wraps her arms around my neck holding me close to her.

Her body trembles against me, as the tears start to flow down her face.

"Graham," she cries, her arms wound tightly. I feel her tears against my neck as trembles rack through her body.

"You're okay. We're both okay," I say to her, doing my best to remain calm even though I feel like I'm about to lose my mind.

She crawls over the seat into my lap and I hold her, doing my best to calm her down. We sit like this for a few minutes, until her tears have dried and her body has stopped shaking.

"I'll drive us the rest of the way to my place."

She nods her head. The adrenaline that was once racing through her has eased and now she's crashing. The exhaustion weighing her down, as her eyes begin to droop.

I move to open the door and she scoots over into the seat. Closing the door behind me, I race to the other side and slip into the driver's seat. I try to make quick work of getting us back to my place. Thankfully, we're not too far now so it only takes a couple of minutes.

Her forehead is pressed against the glass of the window, as she looks out with her body curled up into a ball. Her arms are wrapped tightly around her legs, and I realize now how fragile she looks.

"You ready to head inside?"

It takes a minute before she unwraps herself, looking over at me.

"Graham, I was so scared," she says, as the tears fill her eyes again.

I tell her to hang on a sec as I turn the car off and come around to her side, helping her out. She doesn't hesitate when I wrap my arms around her lower back and her legs, picking her up. She tangles her arms around my neck, holding onto me as I carry her inside.

She helps grab the keys from my pocket and unlocks the door. Kicking the door shut behind me, I don't stop as I take her down the hall and into my bedroom. Setting her on the edge of my mattress, I press a soft kiss against her lips.

"I know you were scared," I whisper to her. "I was scared too."

In fact, I was terrified. Images flash before my eyes of me racing down the side of the road, the gravel crunching beneath my feet as my lungs burned with every deep breath I struggled to take. I envision the red and blue lights from the emergency responders, as I frantically look around for Gage, hoping to see him standing around or being loaded into the ambulance.

I learned painfully that day that he had died at the scene of the accident, and as much as I wished otherwise, they wouldn't be transporting him to the hospital. No, they would be pronouncing him dead at the scene and taking him directly to the morgue.

Watching the ambulance drive away that night without Gage in the back was hard enough to accept. Knowing that I would never see him or talk to him again was a painful reminder that life can change in an instant. Nothing is guaranteed, and in a moment, it can be taken from you.

All this time I felt regretful for what happened to Gage, feeling like it was my actions that put him on the road that night. It was my reckless behavior that made him have to come get me and if it wasn't for me, he would've never been there. He never would've got into that accident.

Now it's a painful reminder that life is too short.

"I don't know what I'd do if something would've happened to you," I say, the thought of losing her causes my voice to crack.

It's now that the tears that were threatening to fall begin their slow descent down her soft cheeks. Wrapping my hands around her face, I press a deep kiss against her lips and hope that without words she feels every emotion pouring out of me and into her. I hope she understands everything I want to say but just can't find the words because I'm so overwhelmed, I just want to hold her. I want to remind myself that she's here with me, and even though we haven't talked about it, I want to believe she's mine.

When our lips break apart, she wraps her hands around my wrists and we just sit here with our foreheads pressed together. Our warm breaths mix together, reminding us that we're both here and alive.

"Will you take a shower with me and then hold me tonight?"

I want to wash away the smell of dirt and exhaust from our bodies and lie together, with her wrapped in my arms.

"Of course," I say, grabbing her by the hand and leading her into the bathroom located off my bedroom suite.

We don't say a word as we both help undress each other. With every piece of clothing that is stripped away, I feel like every wall that's been built up between us falls away too.

Standing here together, under the water steadily falling from the shower, I wrap my arms around her and just appreciate the feel of her skin against mine.

Halle presses a soft kiss against my chest, just over my heart as she circles her arms around my waist. When she peers up at me now, it's like my heart stops beating for a moment, when I see the love on her face shining back at me.

Then when the words that follow pass her lips, I want to fall to my knees and wrap my arms around her waist, just thanking God and heaven for this woman.

"I love you."

I don't know what I've done to deserve her. I don't deserve her one bit. Her light and her goodness, she's everything that's right in this cruel world.

When I tell her I love her back, I kiss her with so much passion I let myself believe for a moment I do deserve her. Lord knows, I wish I did. With every ounce that's left in me, I wish I deserved her, and I vow to spend the rest of my life trying to prove to her I do.

chapter twenty-three

HALLE

A soft grunting sound pulls me out of my sleep, jolting me awake. I stare wide-eyed around the room. My dream is blurring with reality and for a moment, I find myself disoriented and unsure of where I am until Graham's arm tightens around me.

"You okay?" His warm breath feathers over my ear, a piece of hair draping over my face.

Turning in his arms to face him, taking in the sleepy look on his face. His hair is mussed, and his facial hair has grown in longer than he normally wears it, giving him this rugged look that is so very sexy.

"I'm better now." I smile, running my fingers through his wayward hair. His eyes droop, relaxing.

When we were younger, Graham would often sneak in through my bedroom window when my parents were asleep. While it certainly wouldn't have made them happy had they known, there was always a sense of peace that fell over me having his arm wrapped around me. Waking up this morning in his arms is the same. Even with the events of this past week, there is still a calmness I feel being with Graham that I've never been able to find anywhere else.

"You doin' okay after last night?"

"Yeah, I think so."

Graham's long eyelashes feather out over his face as he blinks. Even as he looks back at me with a warm smile, I can tell his mind is somewhere further away.

"I was thinking last night when we were lying in bed," I sigh. "What is it about you that has Krate so hell bent in pissing you off?"

Graham moves his arm, rolling onto his back. Shoving the pillow up, he drapes his arm underneath his head looking up at the ceiling.

"Couldn't tell ya," he responds curtly. His tone is completely different than it was just a moment ago.

Rolling onto my stomach, I sit up and face him, my eyes blazing into the side of his face not buying it for a second.

"You have no idea why he would try to chase us down and practically run us off the road?"

His eyes dart over to me out of the corner of his eye, before closing them and letting out a heavy sigh.

"You're going to make me do this, aren't you?"

"Graham, tell me what's wrong."

"Shortly after I got into town, I got a call from Detective Keller." The mere mention of his name has me sitting up. Folding my legs under me, I pull the blanket over my lap as Graham wraps his hand in mine.

"He called me and asked me to stop by the station. I figured it had to do with Gage, but I hadn't been expecting what he had to tell me. Around the time the accident happened, Gage had been working on a case. Do you remember how news broke about the big drug sting that landed Isaac Krate in prison?"

He must read the question on my face, as I nod my head. What do Isaac Krate and Gage have to do with the accident?

Graham pulls my hand toward him, pressing a soft kiss against my palm before resting our joined hands against his chest.

"It turns out Gage had been taking the lead on the case. Maverick and I have been digging into it and we found out Gage had been the one who had been by to question him. He was helping build the case against him. Anyway, after he was caught and put away, it pissed some people off. Turns out the sting brought down some of their biggest men. Marc clearly didn't like how Gage had been coming around. It's unclear what all he had on them, but they think the accident was done out of retaliation. Maverick and I believe he may have been trying to cover something up, but we can't be certain."

"You think Marc is who's responsible for the hit and run?"

"According to Keller, that's what their leads have come to, but they don't have solid evidence built around it yet."

It's all piecing together now. It's starting to make sense why Marc has been warning Graham and his guys to stay away from him. They are looking for something on him.

"Graham, don't you think if he's willing to risk hurting Gage that he's willing to do more to get you to leave him be? You should leave it alone. Let the cops handle this."

I can hear the panic in my voice just thinking about Graham being on the receiving end of the same fate. I won't lose him, not again.

"Hey," Graham says, sitting up pulling me by my arm.

Pushing the blanket aside, I climb over his legs and into his lap. Tears well up in my eyes as thoughts come flying through my mind. Thinking back to last night, what if something had happened to us when we were driving too? What if he ran us off the road and Graham got hurt, or worse?

What if he did something that took him away from me?

"It's okay, please don't cry."

"No, it's not okay. It's not. You have to stop, don't you understand? He's already said once if you don't back off, he's going to put you six feet under next to Gage. Don't you get it? He has already told you he will do the same. He's practically admitting it."

"Him threatening it doesn't mean he's guilty, Halle. I need to do right by him. It's my fault he was there that night. It's my responsibility to see that Gage gets justice."

Holding Graham's face between my hands, I force him to look at me.

"You may be the reason he was on the road that night, but what happened to Gage is not your fault."

Graham jerks his head away, turning away from me. I sense he doesn't believe me, and it pisses me off he's putting this on himself.

"Damn it, Graham. Look at me."

He pushes me off his lap and moves to stand. I'm taken aback this is how he's reacting, hating he's once again pushing me away.

"You know what, never mind. I'm going to get dressed, you can take me home."

Graham charges toward me, pulling me back to him, and forcing me to turn to look at him.

"Halle, don't."

"You don't want to talk about it, then fine. I don't want to be here. Just take me home so I can get ready for work."

"Fuck," he responds, frustrated, running his hand through his hair. His arms are broad, the move making his muscles flex. My mind quickly moves in a different direction, thinking about all the ways his strong arms will have their way with me if I don't listen. He looks so damn sexy.

That knowledge only makes me more frustrated. Arguing with him is infuriating because even when I'm mad, I still want to climb up his body and have my way with him.

"Halle," he warns, seeing the way I'm eyeing him.

Staring up at him, I force myself not to think about my attraction to him. Sex isn't going to cover up or solve the problems we have like they did the night of the wedding. We need to talk about this if we have any hope of moving forward.

Closing the distance between us, I wrap my arms around his middle. With my face pressed against his chest, I hear the steady beat of his heart and I focus on that sound.

It's a reminder he's still here with me, he's still alive.

"It's not your fault," I mumble.

He brings his arms up, wrapping them around my shoulder. He drops his face down next to mine, pressing a kiss against my collarbone.

"I know," he says, and my body deflates hearing the words as he steps away. "It doesn't mean I don't feel guilty still.

Maybe if he hadn't been on the road, it would've happened eventually. Maybe the outcome would've been different."

"Or maybe it wouldn't have been. Graham, you can sit here all day and speculate over the could've beens, but it isn't going to change what happened. I wish it were different, but Gage wouldn't want you to do this to yourself."

"Maybe not, but he would want answers. He would want justice."

I nod in agreement. He's right.

"You're right, he would. Gage was smart, strong, and honorable. He fought for what was right, and he would be proud of the man you've become."

My heart hammers in my chest, heaving with every word. I'm so frustrated and confused. My head is all over the place right now.

"Halle," Graham says, pulling me out of my thoughts. "I love you."

Just like that, nothing else matters.

"I love you too."

He reaches out, grabbing my hand and pulls me closer. This time I come to him easily, without a fight or arguing. There is nowhere else in this world I'd rather be.

He runs his hand over my cheek, rubbing his thumb along my lower lip. The intensity in his eyes staring back at me, I know he can feel this too.

"Promise me you won't turn your back on me when I'm being stupid, and I'll promise you I'll never leave you again."

"I never turned my..." he stops me, pressing a kiss against my lips.

"Don't argue with me, Halle. Not about this."

"Okay," I say, sliding my hand up into his hair. I pull on the strands, because despite the fact I am not arguing with him, I'm still frustrated.

He moans in response, his hands pressing into me holding me tighter to him. Running my hand down over his jaw, I grab hold of his chin.

Leaning back, I look into his eyes. "I love you, Graham. More than you can possibly imagine. I've never turned my back on you, even when I've been mad or angry. I've been here all along. I was just waiting for the day you would come home to me."

chapter twenty-four

GRAHAM

I ended up driving Halle to work this morning. Dropping her off wasn't easy to do. All morning I was dreading the thought of being away from her, but I knew she would hate it if I asked her not to go. On top of it, there were some things I needed to get done at the office.

After the run-in with Krate on our way home from the races, something told me I needed to drive by and check things out. It's one thing to come after me, to provoke me, but it's another thing completely when you come after the people I love. I wasn't going to sit by idly anymore and let him scare Halle.

He was hiding something. That much is certain. Whatever it is, he doesn't want us to catch onto him. If there's any chance for me to get justice for Gage, I need to figure out what it is.

Checking the rearview mirror, I look to see if anyone is behind me as I glance around the desolate fields surrounding the Krate property. Up until now, no one has been able to prove it, but when Isaac Krate was arrested, Gage had to have known this wasn't going to make people happy. He played a key role in the drugs that passed through Iowa. Stopping him was going to have serious ramifications to their operation.

It's no surprise that with Isaac behind bars it left a spot open for someone to fill his shoes. It wouldn't be long before Marc would be involved in the same bullshit that got them arrested before. Isaac was likely running low on funds and with four children, he needed a way to provide for his family when he was locked up.

Pulling onto the dirt road that leads to the back of the property, I hit the button on the radio as I drive slowly toward the large warehouse that doubles as their residence. Word around town is they use it to hide a lot of their business dealings.

Parking my pickup off behind an old rundown barn, I reach into my pocket and turn my phone on silent. The last thing I need while I'm out here poking around is my cover blown.

I leave the key in the ignition and climb out of the truck, careful not to make any noise as I close the door. When I laid in bed last night, I thought an awful lot about Krate and what would possess him to run us down like he did. His encounters with Halle, along with the fire at my mom's just seem too coincidental to me.

He's up to something and it's time I do something about it, before someone seriously gets hurt. I'd rather it be me than either of them. I grab my pistol from my glove box and check the barrel, before slipping it into the waistband of my pants.

I'd hate to have to use it, but I've learned all too well that these fuckers don't play nicely. If I have to protect myself, I can, and I will.

Jogging across the dirt road, I keep my body pressed up against the side of the warehouse, as I walk along the side of the large building. Leaning my back up against the wall, I listen quietly for any sounds on the other side, before I peek into the window of the door.

It's dark inside and difficult to make out anything. The window almost appears to be tinted, like they don't want anyone to be able to look through. The door is locked, but by the looks of the door frame, it's evident I'm not the first to try and break in. Checking around me again, I use every ounce of force in me to shove the door open.

Grabbing the gun from my waistband, I release the safety and prepare to shoot in the event someone heard me as I quietly close the door behind me. I don't trust any of these fuckers as far as I can throw them. Looking around the room, it's piled high from floor to ceiling with boxes upon boxes.

I don't know what I thought I'd find in here, but unless I plan on going through these, I'm afraid I'm shit out of luck. I open the top of one of the boxes and shuffle through them. It turns up a dead end, only a few kids' clothes. There's another next to it containing some toys and books.

Not wasting my time, I close them as I pull out my flashlight and hold it up looking around the back wall. There's an old rustic workbench that looks like it hasn't been used in years by the layers of saw dust left piled on it.

Stepping over more boxes, I continue to walk toward the other side of the building, noticing several boxes stacked high. Despite that, I spot the metal shining back at me reflecting off the flashlight. I recognize those wheels, they look awfully like the ones Krate has on his old GTO he's driving now.

"What the hell?" I mutter to myself, as I push the boxes to the side and slip between them. The boxes seem to be stacked strategically around the car, so if you were standing at the front of the building you would never see it parked back here.

Sliding the gun back into the waistband of my pants, I hold the flashlight in my mouth as I work to slide the cloth cover off the top of the car.

How the hell would he get the car in and out of here in such a short amount of time? It doesn't make sense.

Dropping the cloth on the dirty cement floor, I hold the flashlight up again as I walk around the back of the black GTO. I flash it into the window, as I round the side toward the front. As the light flashes against the hood of the car, images flash in front of my eyes again.

This time I'm not sitting in the car with Halle, reassuring her and urging her to drive faster. I'm in the moment with Gage, with my phone pressed against my cheek as he yells at me about someone riding his ass.

He looks frantically in his rearview mirror, watching the lights swerve behind him as someone drives erratically. I can feel his heart pumping as the car swerves in the lane next to him, the realization of who it is when he sees the dark GTO keeping the pace just before crashing into him, sending him fishtailing into the ditch.

Shuffling along the side of the car, something tells me to look at the front of the car. Flashing a light over the front fender, my throat goes dry at what I find.

My phone vibrates in my pocket. Maverick's name flashes across the screen. I want to let it go to voice mail, but after what I found I decide against it.

"Mav," I answer.

"Man, where are you at?"

His voice on the other end sounds panicked, setting off alarm bells in my head.

"I'm over at the Krate compound."

"Graham, you need to get out of there. Right now."

"What's going on?"

"Krate found the GPS. The last ping was over an hour ago before it went dark. It took me a minute to figure out where he was at. Graham, did you take Halle home last night after the races?"

"No, she came home with me."

"Well, the last ping came from her apartment. I drove by her place; both her and Kinsley's cars are gone. I believe Kinsley stayed with Wes after the races last night."

"I dropped Halle off at work this morning, her car is still at my place but he's nowhere to be found. I'm leaving here now. I'll call Halle. Do me a favor and get a hold of Kinsley. Tell her to stay with Wes. Do whatever you gotta do to get her to stay away from the salon. After that, I need you to go by my mom's and check on her. This isn't sitting well with me right now."

"On it. What'd you find over at Krate's?" he asks, referring to my comment earlier.

"It's him, man. He was the one that caused Gage's accident. We have him. Motherfucker, we have him. Now we just need to make sure they're safe."

We disconnect the call and my body is shaking with adrenaline. Snapping pictures of the front fender of the wrecked GTO along with a video, showing around the front along with the license plate. I want an insurance policy in case anything were to happen before making a mad dash out of the warehouse toward my pickup.

Once the file saves, I fumble with my phone trying to call Halle. The call repeatedly rings and goes to voice mail, leaving a ball of uneasiness in the pit of my stomach. Trying for a fifth time, the phone immediately goes to voice mail and I know something isn't right.

Turning the key in the ignition, I flip a U-turn and speed off down the dirt road back toward the highway. I'm still about five to seven minutes away, which feels like an eternity.

My phone vibrates again in my hand. My eyes dart to the screen, hoping on a prayer that it's Halle calling me back. I see a text message flash on my screen from Maverick that Kinsley is already off work today, followed by another saying he's headed over to my mom's to check on her and he'll meet me at the salon.

I thank God we live in a small town, where on any day it takes no time to get to where you need to be.

Flying down main street near the salon, I pull into the alley and park in the back. I breathe a sigh of relief for a moment, until I see the black GTO parked alongside the building, and my blood turns to ice in my veins.

I tell myself repeatedly everything's okay. My mind races through a series of thoughts, wondering if maybe Halle forgot to charge her phone last night and that's why she didn't answer, to what I will do if he is here.

For a moment, I consider how I'd handle it if something were to happen to Halle before I quickly push that thought out of my mind. I won't let myself go there, not with her, because if something were to happen to Halle, I don't think I'd live through it.

Reaching the back door of the building, I opt to enter through the employee entrance. It goes into the side door leading into the supply room the girls use.

Slipping inside, I see Halle's purse and apron hanging on the hook near the doorway. Seeing her purse is here, I know she hasn't left, and I breathe a small sigh of relief knowing she's here.

The silence rings loud in my head, until I hear Halle's scared voice say something I never would want to hear.

"You're not going to kill me, are you?"

I listen for any sign of where they might be. Slowly, I turn the knob on the door, I push it shut quietly. Reaching for the gun, I press my back against the wall.

"I haven't decided just yet."

His sinister voice causes the knot in the pit of my stomach to tighten.

I want so badly to wrap my hands around his throat, cutting off his airway as I watch the life drain out of him. The pain I want to inflict on him after what he's done to my family has me thinking the most sinister thoughts.

"Why are you doing this? Why do you keep trying to come after me? Whatever this is between you and Graham, I don't have anything to do with it."

"Stop asking questions!" he shouts at her, followed by a loud smack.

I hear Halle cry out, as she whimpers in pain. *Motherfucker.*

The demons living inside me welcome the chance to dance with the devil. I'll look him in the eye, forcing him to pay for the pain he's inflicted on the people I love.

chapter twenty-five

HALLE

He rears back, smacking me across my cheek with the side of his gun. The pain is so severe it radiates up my jaw causing my ears to ring.

My eyes squeeze shut, wincing and whimpering from the pain. Tears fill my eyes, threatening to fall. Remembering what Graham shared with me, I let the realization sink in that it may have been the last time I will ever see him.

The thought of never touching him or holding him again washes over me like a cold shower. My heart aches, more painful than any pain he could inflict on me.

I don't want to live in a world without Graham Shaw.

Adjusting my position in the chair, the ties around my wrist cut into my skin. It's a welcome distraction away from the reality around me.

I replay the look on Graham's face this morning when he told me he loved me, over and over. Graham deserves justice for Gage. He deserves to move on with his life knowing what happened to him, to put the past to rest once and for all.

My eye starts to swell as the taste of blood seeps into my mouth where my lip split. The coppery taste gives me a renewed sense of anger over everything he's put me and the people I care about through. Not only has Graham suffered, but Sandy and her sister, Gage's mom, Samantha.

They deserve justice too.

"Why did you do it?"

Glancing up under the puffiness of my eye, I see him stop from where he paces the floor and turns to me, sneering.

"What's that?"

"Gage. We know it's you who ran him off the road that night. Why'd you do it?"

The sinister smile returns to his face. Holding the gun against his side, he walks over toward me, skidding his heels along the tile floor as he does. There's a cocky arrogance in his strut and it only infuriates me more as he bends closer to me.

"I thought I told you to stop asking fucking questions!" he shouts, spit shooting from his mouth as each word is punctuated with a stomp of his leather boot.

He stares at me straight in the eyes, as if daring me to utter another word. When he's satisfied I've got the point, he stands up straight and turns to walk away.

"Where the hell is he?" he mutters, pulling back the edge of the blinds to look out the window.

I see a flash of movement from the stockroom across from me. My eyes widen with fear, before I see Graham appear. He holds a finger up to his mouth, telling me to stay quiet. My eyes dart back over to Krate, standing a few feet away with his back to Graham, before looking back to Graham.

He mouths to me it will be okay and I nod, feeling for the first time since Krate got here it will be.

I had a feeling it was Graham who called me earlier. When my phone rang repeatedly, Krate took it from me smashing it on the ground in front of me before stomping on it.

My hands tug on the confines again, wishing with everything in me I could loosen them and run to Graham, wrapping my arms around him.

Krate pulls out his phone, checking the screen. Taking his attention off me opens the perfect opportunity for Graham to catch him off guard, and he does.

"If I were you, I'd put the gun down right now," Graham says, pointing a gun at Krate.

The sound of Graham's voice catching him off guard, causes him to drop his phone, as he readjusts the aim back at me.

Krate smiles broadly, the light cackling sound of his laughter filling the room. It's evil, sending a chill down my spine.

"I was waiting on you. It was only a matter of time till you'd swoop in to save the day. You're never far behind this one."

Graham's jaw ticks, my eyes flash back and forth between the two of them. I want to beg Graham to be careful, but the anger simmering below the surface is evident by the wild look in his eyes.

"You just couldn't listen, could ya? Just had to keep sticking your nose where it don't fuckin' belong. Your cousin had the same problem, ya know. It's a shame you'll have to lose someone you love again."

"If you hurt her, I promise you as God as my witness, I'll kill you. I won't even think twice about it either. This is your only warning. So, think long and hard over the next move you make."

There's no threat in Graham's words. It's a promise, spoken with such conviction. It's one he fully intends to keep if he's pushed to that point.

Krate chuckles, the sound grating like nails on a chalkboard.

"You should never threaten a man who has nothing to lose."

The sound of sirens in the distance grows closer as Krate adjusts his aim at me. Anger transforms his face.

"Hate to say it," Graham says. "It looks like it's you this won't be ending well for."

Graham shouts for me to duck, just as the sound of shots fire around the room. The mirror on the salon station behind me breaks, sending glass shattering around me, as Graham rushes Krate.

The weight of Graham's heavy frame and the blast from his gun sends Krate stumbling, falling back against the wall. I fold my body in half, pressing my chest to my knees, protecting myself.

"Why'd you do it?" Graham grunts, forcing his elbow against Krate's neck, cutting off his airway. Graham's eyebrow is cut deep, leaving blood trickling down his forehead.

"Fuck you," Krate spits.

"You had your chance," Graham growls, rearing back elbowing him in the face. Blood splatters from his nose just before Graham hits him with a heavy fist against his jaw. I watch as life leaves Krate's body with every blow.

"Graham!" I shout, pulling him out of it. He pushes off his body, holding his hands up as he kicks Krate's gun away from him.

The front door slams open as several men rush in, shouting "police." Graham falls to the floor before me, holding his hands in the air.

He looks dazed, lost. His body shaking, a mixture of fear and adrenaline coursing through him. His eyes look me over, checking for any sign I could be hurt.

"I'm okay, I promise. I'm okay."

I say it over and over, never taking my eyes off him. After the fourth or fifth time, he lets out a deep sigh finally accepting it as the truth.

I hear someone say "all clear" as another person identifies Graham. As soon as the all clear is given, Graham slides across the floor on his knees until his forehead is pressed against mine.

"I love you," he whispers. "Fuck, I don't know what I would've done if something happened to you."

He looks up, tears in his eyes, focusing on something behind me, before looking back down at me.

"You two okay?" Maverick asks, appearing next to us out of nowhere.

"Get something to untie her," Graham orders, just as Detective Keller approaches us. Mav produces a knife from his pocket and quickly releases me of the restraints. My wrists cry from the pain.

"You're lucky you didn't get yourself shot. We found enough ammunition in his car to do some serious damage. What were you doing coming in here by yourself and not waiting for us to arrive?" Keller questions.

"With all due respect, there's nothing I wouldn't do to make sure that woman was okay."

"Well, if it's alright with you, I'm going to have her taken to the hospital to get checked out. Make sure there's nothing wrong. We'll meet you up there to get her statement."

"I'm okay," I say, looking back at Graham shaking my head.

"She's okay. If it's alright with you, I'd like to just get her out of here."

Glancing over, I see them loading up Krate on a stretcher with his hand clutching his shoulder. I want to be angry all he is left with was a gunshot to his shoulder and a busted-up face when Gage lost his life, but I know he'll be in prison for a long time.

"Alright. We'll be by your place to talk to you. I will just need your information," Keller says, looking at me.

"I can get you that information," Maverick says, interjecting. "I'll let Graham get her out of here, if it's alright with you."

"You can just come by my place. She'll be with me."

The next few days are a blur. After we left the salon, we went back home and later that evening the detectives came over to Graham's to question us. I knew Marc and Isaac Krate had been involved in what happened to Gage but hearing about Graham finding the car was bone chilling.

There was no denying after what he said that day in the salon, the warnings he's given both me and Graham to back off, and finding the car he was responsible for Gage's death.

What happened afterward was the first big step Graham needed in getting the justice Gage deserved. The night we found out that charges had been filed and Marc wouldn't be released on bail, this was the first night Graham was able to sleep.

As for me, the only time I've been able to get any rest is when I've had Graham's arms around me. We never discussed it, but we both knew without needing to talk about it that we needed each other right now.

Having lost Graham once before, I felt the fear of losing him and saw life without him again flash before my eyes.

Waking up the next morning with the sound of rain pattering outside the window and Graham's soft breathing behind me is its own piece of heaven. I remind myself to appreciate the little things in life. These are the moments I won't take for granted again.

"Good morning," I whisper, as Graham presses a kiss against my shoulder.

Rolling over in his arms, I smile at his sleepy eyes. His facial hair has grown out longer, having not shaved over the past few days.

"Morning," he croaks, as I reach up and run my palm over his cheek.

He closes his eyes at my touch, as I run my thumb over his face. I feel him jolt in surprise when I lean over, pressing a soft kiss against his lips.

"I love you," I whisper against his lips. His body relaxes, as he reaches down to grab my leg, curving it over his so our legs tangle together.

He doesn't say anything but when his eyes open, the evidence is there. The love shining back at me nearly takes my breath away as his lips press against mine, this time with more force and conviction. His hands run up my forearms, holding me closer to him.

When his tongue skims over my bottom lip, seeking entrance, I give into him. Every damn time I give into him. I can feel everything he's saying to me, but the connection between us is so deep, there are no words necessary.

Pressing his forehead to mine, he breaks the connection. Tilting his head back, he looks at me for a moment before whispering, "I love you too."

Tears fill my eyes and his brows furrow with confusion and concern.

"What's wrong, baby?"

"I'm just so happy to hear you say those words again," I say, my voice quivering with every word spoken.

"After so much time passed after you left, I never thought I'd see you again. If I did, I never expected we would be together. All the time we were apart didn't change how much I love you. I was scared I was going to lose you and, God, I don't think I'd ever be able to get through it again."

"Halle," he replies, cutting me off. The soft voice he used a moment ago gone and the take charge man is back in its place. "You will never lose me again."

"But what if," I say, before he interjects.

"Hear me, Halle. You won't ever lose me. I'm yours."

"Promise?"

"Until my last breath."

A tear slips out of my eyes, trailing down my face, as he continues.

"I know what I did hurt you, but I need you to understand, walking away from you was the biggest mistake I've ever made in my life. I won't let myself make it again. I am so in love with you and the thought of living without you again, I won't do it. It won't happen. I want to wake up every morning with you in my arms. I'll spend every day for the rest of our lives proving to you I'm not going anywhere. Not now. Not ever."

If I was emotional before, I'm in full on ugly cry now. Everything he just said to me is what I've longed to hear from him.

We can't go back and change the past. If we could, there are many things I'm sure we'd love to re-write. All we can do now is focus on the here and now, and everyday forward. Just knowing he wants to wake up with me in my arms is all I needed to hear, but everything else sealed the deal.

epilogue

GRAHAM
three months later

"You nervous, man?"

I glance over at Brannon and his shit eating grin spreads wide across his face. The fucker knows I'm nervous, which is why he's even bothering asking right now.

"Shut up," I growl, earning me a laugh.

"It's about time you wised up already. Five years, dude—took you long enough. That girl's a ten, man. I'm glad you came to your senses."

"I could say the same to you, asshole. Why don't you shut your mouth?"

He stops, looking at me confused, and I laugh back at him. "What are you talking about?"

"Lissa," I respond, drawing it out. He has the gall to stare at me, continuing to look confused.

"We all know what happened in Chicago. The look on your face, the one saying you don't know what I'm talking about, isn't going to get you anywhere."

He doesn't respond right away, instead takes a throwback of what's left in his can of beer. Come to think of it, I'm certain I just saw him up at the bar not even five minutes before this, so he has to be chugging the entire thing.

Slamming the empty can down on the table, he looks back at me. I know my response grinded his nerves, if the annoyed look on his face is any indication. I wasn't trying to be an asshole about it, just proving the point that we don't always know what's right in front of our face.

"Whatever you think you know, I ain't chasin' that girl around. Not anymore. That ship sailed."

"Uh huh." I laugh. "Do me a favor, when we look back on this conversation a year from now, we can both shake hands in agreement knowing we told the other so. Fair?"

"Whatever, man. I need another beer. You want one? You know, to work up the courage and all that."

"Fuck off," I retort, as he raises his hand in salute walking away.

My leg starts to shake. The nervous energy coursing through me heightened.

Three months ago, everything changed. Call me stupid, or perhaps if you ask Brannon maybe I just wised up. Either way, I know what it was like to lose Halle once when I mistakenly walked away. I told myself it was the right decision. I was clouded by the guilt of what happened to Gage, and I let it push her away.

I won't make that mistake again. I made her a promise to spend every day working to earn her trust and showing her how much I love her. I fully intend to keep my promise.

Looking at the back door, I wait for her to come in. She texted me ten minutes ago telling me she and Kinsley had closed the salon and were on their way. Mason, Brea, Callum, and Ellie are all here already. Everyone knows the plan.

Everyone, except for Halle that is.

The ring in my pocket is starting to burn a hole through the denim. I'm so nervous and anxious to see her, to see her face, and get this over with already.

I just want to know she's mine forever.

She left earlier this morning, she had an appointment to get to before she had to work. I feel like it's been too long since I've seen her and I'm ready to just have her in my arms and to kiss her.

Fuck, Brannon is right, I'm glad I came to my senses.

It feels like ten minutes goes by, but for all I know it's probably been more like two, when Halle bounds through the door. Her long blonde hair is curled over her shoulder and the denim jeans are hugging every curve of her body like they were made for her.

Damn, I swear this woman could bring me to my knees.

When her eyes find mine across the bar, I can't help but grin when I see them light up. Her smile is so damn bright, it's a wonder what I did to have her.

"Hey, baby." I smile, reaching out for her hand and pulling her into my arms.

"Well, hello there, handsome."

I don't hesitate, I lean forward and press a kiss against her lips. Her hand wraps around the front of my shirt, I hold myself closer to her.

"I missed you."

"You saw me this morning." She giggles.

"So, that was nine hours ago. Too damn long."

"What would you do without me?"

"I don't know, but I don't want to find out."

"Good answer." She smiles, pushing up on her toes to reach for another kiss. Wrapping my hands around her waist, I hold her close to me.

"You two need to get a room already!" Mason shouts from behind us.

Ignoring him, I pick her up by her waist and she wraps her legs around me, which earns us a laugh.

"I feel like we're back in high school all over again," Kinsley mutters from behind us.

We finally break away and I smile seeing the way Halle's face lights up.

"You hear that?"

"I did."

"We're young and in love all over again."

"Never stopped."

Her face softens hearing that as I lower her back to the floor.

I look around at the group of my friends, all of them eagerly waiting for the moment that's about to come. It's ironic, really. The nerves that were once surging through me a few minutes ago are now gone, and a sense of calmness washes over me.

This is exactly where I was supposed to be, with these people, all along.

When my eyes fall on Kinsley's, she nods her head toward me, encouraging me to get on with it already. She's so happy, her excitement is bubbling beneath the surface.

"I want to thank you all for joining us here tonight," I say, as Halle turns her head looking up at me.

"It's no secret the past few years haven't always been easy for me. For any of us. We've all been through our own fair share of hard times, but I know I couldn't get through it without all of you."

Pulling Halle around so she's turning to face me, she smiles, squeezing my hand.

"Halle, I promised you I was never going to leave you again. I meant what I said. Coming home to you was the second-best thing I've done in my life."

Leaning forward, I press a kiss against her lips. She reaches her hand out, holding her palm against my face as I pull back to look at her again.

"If it's alright with you, I'd like to get on with making the best one." Her brows furrow in question, just before I lower myself to my knee. Her eyes widen as tears fill her eyes.

"Don't cry." I smile, pressing a kiss against the back of her hand.

I hear the girls cry out, saying something about how sweet I am.

"Baby, I've been in love with you since the moment you first smarted off to me." I pause, loving the sound of her laugh as I say that. "I want to spend every day of my life showing you just how much. Help me make the best damn decision I've ever made in my life and marry me. There's not a damn person in this world I want to spend my life with but you. Will you be my wife?"

"Oh my God," she cries, straddling my bended knee as she presses her lips against mine. I wrap my arms around her, holding her to me.

Tears flow down her face, mixing with our kisses.

"Baby, I told you not to cry. Why you cryin'?"

"You make me so damn happy."

"Well, that's good. I was starting to wonder what was wrong. You still haven't given me an answer yet."

She stands back up, laughing as she looks around our group of friends before looking back down at me.

"You want my answer, Graham Shaw?"

I nod my head, smiling.

"Yes, I'll marry you. I want to be your wife and the mother of your children. It's about time you made an honest woman out of me."

It takes me a second to piece together what she's trying to say, as gasps erupt from around us.

"Halle..." I say, stopping. My heart feels like it's going to beat out of my chest now.

"Well, considering I'm pregnant with your child and all."

My arms wrap around her, lifting her off the floor. When I finally set her down, I can't stop kissing her. She jumps up and down excitedly, as I slip the diamond ring over her finger.

"I'm marrying the sexiest damn DILF in Arbor County!" Halle shouts, holding her hand in the air waving her ring at her friends.

"Yay!" Kinsley yells. She rushes over to hug us both, sighing in relief over how she's glad she doesn't have to keep it a secret anymore.

"It was only one day."

"It felt like forever," Kinsley sighs dramatically.

Everyone else around us cheers and claps, coming over to hug us. Ellie is standing next to us, with Callum's arms around her, helping console his wife who is in full-on tears.

This is what it's all about. Family, friends, and the love of my life. Until I found Halle, I didn't know what true happiness was.

Now, that I've found it, I won't ever let her go.

Thank you for reading **UNTIL I FOUND YOU**! I hope you loved Graham and Halle as much as I do.

You can continue the Heart's Compass series with <u>Now That I Found You</u>, a continuation of Callum and Ellie's story.

If you loved Until I Found You, I appreciate your help in spreading the word, including telling a friend. Reviews help readers find books! Please leave a review on your favorite site.

You can sign up for my newsletter to learn more about my new releases. You can also join my Facebook group, Brooke O'Brien's Rebel Reader Group, for exclusive giveaways and sneak peeks of future books. To join, please visit:

www.authorbrookeobrien.com/follow.

Now, turn the page for a sneak peek of Now That I Found You...

NOW THAT I *found you*

A HEART'S COMPASS
BOOK FOUR

USA *TODAY* BESTSELLING AUTHOR
BROOKE O'BRIEN

prologue

ELLIE

I've always believed the people we grow into are a result of the challenges we've faced and the lessons we've learned throughout our lives. The decisions we make guide us down different paths, leading us to destinations we had never planned or expected for ourselves. While there's always a little bit of God's hand and fate at play, it's ultimately our decisions that lead us to where we end up.

I still remember the day I met Callum, standing outside the bus station in the pouring rain. The heartbreak I had lived through leading me to make the difficult decision to leave my small town of Garwood. It was one of many choices I had been forced to make at such a young age.

I fell for him all over again the night at Brodie's when I saw the sparkle in his eye and the rebellious grin he wore on his face. He made it so hard for me to stay away from him, even though I knew the risks of letting him in.

I know with all my heart he was brought into my life with the purpose of showing me there are people in this world who will protect me and love me, scars and all. Marrying him was the best decision I've ever made in my life. When I stop and allow myself to think about it, I smile knowing my dad had a hand in bringing Callum to me.

I found a family here in Arbor Creek and a place I can finally call home. For the first time, I'm allowing myself to picture a life I never thought I could have. One that I always thought was out of reach for me.

All I've ever wanted was a family of my own. But like everything in my life, I should've known the road ahead wasn't going to be easy for the two of us. Life has always had its way of testing me. Our future is about to change in ways we never expected, and one man's decisions threaten to take everything I've always wanted away from me again.

chapter one

CALLUM
august

"You almost ready, baby?" I ask, as I lightly tap my knuckles on the door. Leaning in closer, I listen for signs of movement on the other side.

The sound of Ellie's heels clicking on the tile floor of our hotel suite brings a smile to my face. Just the mental image of seeing her in her summer dress, getting ready, knowing how beautiful she looks.

Running my hand over my button-up shirt, I step back when I hear the footsteps approaching before the door handle is turned and she's standing before me.

Her hair has a light wave to it, brighter than it was just a week ago. Her tan skin is bronzer and there's a light dusting of freckles appearing over the apples of her cheeks. They are rosy from the sun she got when we were lying out on the beach earlier today.

Glancing down, I take in my wife standing in front of me. She looks like a fucking angel in her white dress. It cuts into a deep V, teasing me with what I know she looks like underneath.

Following the path down to her legs to the heels wrapped around her feet, I barely hold back the urge to drop to my knees before her. She's a fucking sight to see. The possessive side of me wants to growl, pull her into my arms, and keep her locked away in our hotel room for the rest of the night.

I don't know how I got so lucky with her, but I won't let her know I question it either. When I see the glistening of the wedding band flashing where it sits on her ring finger, something in me shifts.

She's my wife and despite hating the thought of any other man looking at her, I love knowing she's wearing my ring and showing the world she's mine. That's enough to get me to let go of my overprotectiveness and instead, reach out and grab her hand, pulling her closer to me.

"I'm ready." She giggles, as she falls against my chest. She rubs her palm over my abs, biting her lip as she peers up at me.

"Don't look at me like that, Ellie."

There's a sparkle in her eye at my comment as a light smirk lines her lips. It distracts me, I swear she leaves me constantly hanging on the edge with want. I could so easily close the distance between us and kiss her mouth.

"Like what?" She feigns innocence, which on any other day I might actually believe, but right now, I know better.

Her tongue darts out, lightly tracing a line over her lip, teasing me. She knows exactly what she's doing. It can't happen right now though. We have a dinner reservation in ten minutes, and I have plans for her, despite how good she looks right now.

"Don't think I don't see through that innocent look, sweetheart. I know you better than that," I growl, kissing her deeply. She hums softly, as she slides her hands up my chest and around my neck, holding me close to her.

I love how confident she's become around me. The once shy and timid girl, held back by her past, doesn't hold herself back anymore. She takes what she wants, and I love how she doesn't suppress her urges when it's me she wants.

Keeping my forehead pressed against hers, I break our kiss and struggle to breathe again.

"We have dinner reservations at eight o'clock. We should get going. If I don't stop us now, we will end up like last night where I'm ordering you room service and feeding you dinner in bed naked again."

She smiles deviously before she nods her head. "We are on our honeymoon after all."

For a minute I think she's ready for me to cancel our plans before she pulls back, lacing her fingers in mine. "We might as well enjoy it while we can. We're married now, which means we'll have many days of naked dinners when we're back home."

I almost consider saying to hell with it, when she turns and pulls me down the hallway of our hotel suite. I get a glimpse of her in this dress from behind, her hair pulled over to the side, showing off the column of her neck, making my cock twitch in my pants.

"Fuck," I mutter to myself, as she squeezes my hand tighter as she looks back at me, biting her lip.

"Let's make this quick then."

Once we're out of the hotel and heading down toward the beach, I'm glad we decided to keep our plans for the evening. The sun has started to set, lighting up the sky in a beautiful array of pink and orange, as the waves crash in the distance. We make it to the end of the dock, leading us to the secluded area I had arranged for us for tonight.

Ellie stops, leaning down to undo the strap around her foot before I bend down in front of her. Unhooking the clasp, I ease her foot out of her heels as she steps down into the sand.

I probably should've asked you if my shoes were appropriate for tonight," she whispers down to me.

Running my hand over her calf down to her ankle, I peer up at her and smile. "Oh, they're always appropriate. I'll show you why later."

She grins, shaking her head at me. "Lord, what am I going to do with you?"

"I can think of a few things." I chuckle.

"Mhmm." She laughs, as I lead her over to the blanket laid out in the sand overlooking the water. When she sees the setup I had arranged for her, she lets out a subtle gasp before she wraps her arms around my waist.

"Callum," she sighs. "I can't believe…" Her voice drifts off, as she looks down at the flowers, along with the picnic basket.

"You did all of this?"

I nod. "Of course, I did."

She rises up onto her toes, and I lean forward, pressing a kiss against her lips. "Thank you."

I've always loved how easy it is to surprise Ellie. She is grateful for every ounce of love you show her, eager to soak it up. It only makes me want to find new ways to express how I feel for her, wanting to put the same look of love and appreciation on her face every day.

She steps back as I lower myself to the ground, helping her down between my legs. Wrapping my arms around her, pulling her close, she reclines against my chest.

"It's so beautiful here, so peaceful," she sighs blissfully, and I'd give anything to grant her this sense of calmness everyday of our lives. She deserves all the happiness in the world.

I nod. "It's everything I hoped it would be for you."

Leaning over, I pull the basket closer to us. Reaching in, I grab the sandwiches I had packed away earlier when Ellie was taking a nap. We sit here, our bodies entwined, eating as we reminisce over our week. Most of our time was spent tangled up together in our room or somewhere near the water.

"I'm not sure I'm ready to leave yet. Can't we just stay here forever?" Ellie murmurs. She shifts her eyes downcast, tossing her napkin back into the basket. I help her clean up everything before she moves to situate herself back in my arms again.

"We still have the rest of the night here. We might as well enjoy what time we have left."

Tilting my head forward, I press a kiss against her shoulder. She's soft and warm from her sunburn, heat radiating from her skin. The moment my lips brush against her, I feel her body tremble beneath my touch.

I've always loved the way she reacts to me. Tracing my tongue over her shoulder, I kiss her again from the base of her neck up toward her jaw.

"Callum," she breathes. Her hands grip my arms tightly, holding me to her.

"Yes, sweetheart?"

She doesn't say anything, the words falling the moment they touch her lips coming out more like a small hiss, just as I press another kiss beneath her ear.

She tilts her head to the side, giving me better access to her, and I dive right in. Her chest rises and falls heavily with each forced breath.

Reaching my hand up beneath the curve of her breast, she rests her head back against my shoulder as my finger brushes over her nipple beading through the chiffon of her dress.

"Oh, God," she whispers. She quickly checks around us, making sure we're still alone.

"No one's here, Ellie, but us. Just you and me. I'd never share you with anyone."

She lets out an audible breath, relaxing again in my arms. She's telling me without words she wants me to continue, and I do.

"Does that feel good?" I exhale against her cheek.

She nods, her tongue darting out, wetting her lips. She uncrosses her legs, leaving them stretched out in front of us. I brush my other hand over her stomach, down to the apex of her thigh, pulling the hem of her dress up enough for me to slip my hand beneath the material.

Her body shutters beneath me as I skim the tip of my finger over the seam of her panties, feeling her wetness seep through.

"Damn, sweetheart," I groan, pressing my mouth against her shoulder once again.

Slipping my finger inside her panties, she lets her leg fall open for me. My cock aches in my pants by how bad she wants this right now. My finger grazes over her swollen clit and she doesn't hold back, unleashing a breathy moan.

I alternate between rubbing her clit, to grazing the edge of her pussy lips, before she begs me to stop teasing her. She shifts her head back, her eyes meeting mine, and I see the hunger in the depths. My girl needs me to give her this and, God, I want to give her everything she wants and so much more.

"C'mere," I mutter, urging her to turn to face me. Her movements are slow, her eyes in a daze, as I quickly unzip my pants. My cock rejoices when I wrap my hand around it, pumping it once, twice.

Her eyes laser into me and what I'm doing. I reach for her, needing to feel her body against mine, when she hesitates for a minute.

"I want to watch you do that," she breathes, sliding her hand between her legs to touch herself. Good lord, she is fucking perfect.

I give her what she wants, rubbing my thumb over the tip of my dick, catching the cum dripping before reaching out and pressing it against her lips. She opens her mouth for me, tasting me, as her eyes light up with fire in the depths.

She ditches her earlier idea and closes the distance between us, rubbing her wetness over me, coating my cock.

She pulls her panties to the side as she moves to slide down over me, keeping me pressed to the hilt.

Her eyes find mine again, and the love I find shining back at me is nearly my undoing. The way she fits so perfectly around me makes my heart beat out of my chest. Having her body pressed against me, it's as if everything makes sense. I'm whole.

Her fingers run through my hair, pulling on the strands as she tilts my head back and captures my lips in a soul-crushing kiss. Her body rocks against mine as my hands wrap tightly around her waist, holding her to me.

She throws her head back. Leaning my head forward, I kiss her neck, feeling her heart beat beneath my lips through every struggled breath she takes.

"Callum," she moans, her grip on my hair tightens, and I know she's close. Her body is wound so tight as her pussy clenches around me.

"Ellie, baby. I want you to come with me. Come, baby," I mutter, just as I lightly bite down on her collarbone.

Her body trembles, as she wraps her arms around my neck collapsing against me. I wrap my arms around her. She doesn't move to break our connection, only moves to circle her legs around my lower back, holding herself closer to me.

When our heart rates both go back to normal, I reach my hand up and brush my thumb over the apple of her cheek as I whisper, "I swear you were made to be loved by me."

Do you want more Callum and Ellie?

Check out Now That I Found You today at:
www.authorbrookeobrien.com/nowthatifoundyou

BOOKS BY BROOKE

A Rebels Havoc Series

Brix
Sins of a Rebel
Tysin
Trey
Madden

Men of Blaze

Personal Foul
Reckless Rebound (Cocky Hero Club)

Tattered Heart Duet

Torn
Tattered

A Heart's Compass Series

Where I Found You
Lost Before You
Until I Found You
Now That I Found You
Where You Belong

Standalones (In order of publication)

Wild Irish

Learn more and purchase your copy at:
www.authorbrookeobrien.com/booksbybrooke

PLAYLIST

(Brooke's writing inspiration mixed in with Halle & Graham's favorites.)

Livin' on a Prayer – Bon Jovi
A Little Bit Stronger – Sara Evans
Every Little Thing – Carly Pearce
Drowns the Whiskey – Jason Aldean feat. Miranda Lambert
How Not To – Dan + Shay
Hurricane – Luke Combs
Kerosene – Miranda Lambert
You Make It Easy – Jason Aldean
All to Myself – Dan + Shay
Speechless – Dan + Shay
Heaven – Kane Brown
There Goes My Everything – Kane Brown

Listen to the Playlist on Spotify at:
www.authorbrookeobrien.com/untilifoundyou

ABOUT BROOKE

USA Today Bestselling author Brooke O'Brien writes steamy and swoon-worthy new adult romances. She's best known for her sports and rock star romances.

Brooke believes a love worth having is worth fighting for, and she brings this into her stories where her characters risk it all for love.

When she isn't writing or falling in love with a new book boyfriend, you can find her spending time with her family, cheering on her favorite sports teams, listening to ASMR, or binge-watching the latest true crime documentary. She loves rockin' a comfy hoodie with leggings and believes the best days include a good nap.

Brooke loves connecting with readers and hopes you'll join her on her social pages or reader group to stay in touch. To follow Brooke and join her newsletter, visit authorbro okeobrien.com/follow.

ACKNOWLEDGMENTS

My Boys – I love you more than anything on this earth. Everything I do is for our family.

Mom, Gram, & Ash – Thanks for always being supportive of this journey. You've pushed me to go after everything I want in life. Love you!

To my AMAZING beta readers – Elizabeth, Ana, Ashley, and Cheryl. Thank you for reading Graham & Halle's story before anyone else, for your honest feedback, and helping me make their story better. I'm so grateful for you! <3

My Rebels Babes – I love being able to connect with all of you in my Reader Group. I feel like I've found a place where I can share with you my triumphs and crazy ideas, as well as catching up with you about everything going on in our daily lives. I'm so grateful to have all your support. To my Release Launch Rebels, thank you for being a part of this one. I'm excited to hear what you think of our man, G.

Kate Jessop – What would I do without you? I don't want to find out. Thank you for being there for me when I need to brainstorm an idea or tell me it's going to be okay when I need to hear it.

Melissa Pötgens – Girl, I'm so thankful for you. You've stuck by me since the beginning, cheering me on every step of the way and loving my characters as much as I do. Thank you for being you. For EVERYTHING!

My editor, Roxane LeBlanc. I always enjoy working with you. Thank you for being honest, patient, and so very helpful to me.

My proofreader, Julie Deaton. You have a fantastic eye for detail, and I appreciate all your help in getting this book polished off. Thank you for everything!

Najla with Najla Qamber Designs, you are so incredibly talented and blow me away with your work. Thank you for designing the most beautiful cover.

To Ena with Enticing Journey, thank you for your support and helping me promote my work. I'm forever grateful!

Lastly, to all the fantastic bloggers and authors who have shown me support throughout this journey. I hope you know how grateful I am for every one of you.

COPYRIGHT

Until I Found You: A Heart's Compass novel
Copyright © 2019 by Brooke O'Brien with Tattered Ink Publishing
All Rights Reserved

No part of this book may be reproduced or transmitted in any form or by any means, electronic or mechanical, including photocopying, recording, or by any information storage and retrieval system without written permissions of the author, except for the use of brief quotations in a review.

This is a work of fiction. Names, characters, places and incidents either are the product of the author's imagination or are used fictitiously. Any resemblance to persons, living or dead, business establishments, events, or locales is entirely coincidental. The author acknowledges the trademarked status and trademark owners of various products referenced in this work of fiction, which has been used without permission. The publication/use of these trademarks is not authorized, associated with or sponsored by the trademark owners.

For information on subsidiary rights, please contact Tattered Ink Publishing at www.authorbrookeobrien.com.

Cover Art and Interior Formatting © Najla Qamber, Najla

<u>Qamber Designs</u>
Cover Photo © Shutterstock
Edited by Rox LeBlanc, <u>Roxs Reads</u>
Proofread by Julie Deaton, <u>Deaton Author Services</u>
Version: BMO08042023